Coin at Sea

Emma Nichols

Text copyright 2013 Emma Nichols

Image Copyright Maridav, 2013
Used under license from Shutterstock.com

eBook formatting by
Indie Pixel Studio
(http://www.indiepixelstudio.com)

All rights reserved. No part of this book may be used or reproduced in any manner whatsoever including Internet usage, without written permission of the author.

Dedication

Becky Carter Nichols, thank you for being there for me throughout this project. I don't know that I would have had the courage, the confidence, or the determination to finish without you.

Can't wait to collaborate on Vixen in Vegas!

Much love to my girls,

JB, Elle, Jodi, Brandelyn, Lorraine, Tammy, and Alexis

Every woman needs friends like all of you!

Chapter 1

I am a runner. Not an actual runner, like with shoes and sweat. Instead, I specialize in leaving uncomfortable situations with alarming speed. Some people need closure; I need space. When I need this space, I do it in style. I keep a variety of emergency credit cards at the ready for such an occasion. This one…was going to require the black card…and my BFF.

Jolie and I have been through it. Every tragedy imaginable and those that most would never want to imagine. She has never failed me. This time would be no different. All I had to do was call. So, I pressed the button on the steering wheel. Damn, I loved Sync.

"Call Jolie on cell."

Seconds later, the phone was ringing and seconds after that, she answered. "What's up, girl!" She shouted in excitement.

"How soon can you be packed and how long can you go?" I asked.

See, the beauty of my life, and Jolie's is that we are digital nomads. We can work from just about anywhere. We can live wherever we want. We don't have an office to go to, a set schedule, or any ties. Hell, I don't even have a plant. I pretty much said screw it after my lucky bamboo died. It was a sign. I took it as such. That was one of the causes of my last move.

"Are we moving or regrouping?" Jolie asked. She was always ready for whatever adventure I instigated…and I have a habit of instigating adventure.

"Let's regroup for a move. How does that sound?" I could feel the tension draining away at merely hearing her voice and letting it all out.

"I take it Kyle fucked up," she said seriously. "What a douche. Wanna tell me all about it now while I pack?

That was my cue. I had been dying for her to be ready for me to unleash. So, I did. "Well, he's been working late so often lately that I thought I'd surprise him by bringing dinner to the office."

"Oh, crap," she said. This is why we're besties. Forever. Jolie always knows how to offer just the right kind of sympathy.

"Yeah. I make it to the office. His car is in the garage. I take the elevator up. When I get in there, he's fucking his secretary on the conference table. It's so…cliché! Who does that?" I took a breath.

"Go on. Tell me you confronted him." She was so encouraging.

"I was furious!"

She chuckled. "I imagine."

"I paced. I waited. It seemed like it was going to be a marathon fuck as opposed to one of his quickies, so finally I sat down on the couch in the waiting area. I laid out the food. I lit the candle." I paused for dramatic effect.

"And you burned the office down!" She sounded just a little too excited at that prospect.

"Nope. Maybe I should have." I thought for a moment. "Nah, I'm too pretty for jail." I joked. It earned me the laugh I intended. "I poured the wine. I sat there and sipped on a glass while I waited. And when they were done and dressed and *she* walked out, I just stared at her."

"Ouch. I hurt for her. You could kill with those looks." I could hear hangers rattling and drawers opening and closing as we spoke. The calm was finally taking hold; I had stopped shaking.

"I wish I could kill with those looks, or at least maim. She had looked so pleased with herself until she saw me there looking all cool and confident on the couch. And that's when Kyle came out. He was tightening his tie and wiping lipstick off his cheek."

"Oh. My. Gawd." She squealed. "What did you say?"

"I told him to enjoy dinner and have a nice life. Then I looked at her and told her she could have my leftovers because I don't share. That's when I stood up and walked out." I sighed.

"Whoa. That's it?" She sounded surprised.

"Hey, I'm a class act. I don't throw punches. I don't throw fits. And I don't give second chances. I'm done. On to the regrouping." I forced a smile. This was actually bothering me more than I let on.

"How soon until you get here?" She asked.

"I'm pulling onto your street now. I'll wait in the car. You know the drill. No more than one bag. We'll buy what we're missing." With that, I hung up the phone, pulled into the driveway and waited. This was the fun part. I loved regrouping. I loved fresh starts. This time, after three years in the same place, I needed a big change. This one was going to be massive. We'd need at least a week or ten days to get it together.

The passenger door opened and she threw her duffle bag in the back seat. It landed next to mine. They were identical bags purchased on our first regroup ten years before soon after we graduated from high school. That was when we became digital nomads…on that trip. We had perfected it. We even had a motto…never settle and never settle down.

The lifestyle, the freedom, the quality time together was perfect for us. We weren't built for routine and normal lives. As I sat there lost in thought, my cell started to ring, since I had given Kyle a custom ring tone, there was no doubt who it was. I didn't even need to look at the screen. He had already called three times while I was on the phone with Jolie and before I had even made it out of the parking garage. This was call number five. He was serious. Hell, he was a lawyer; he was paid to be serious.

Knowing that he would simply keep calling, I decided to answer so that Jolie and I could focus on the good stuff. I motioned for her to remain silent. She nodded, her eyes big happy saucers, eager to become a voyeur in my life. It wouldn't be the first time. I pressed the button on the steering wheel to accept the call. "Kyle, what's up?"

"Alysin, how could you just leave without trying to talk to me? We've been together for two years. I chased you for an entire year before that." He sounded frantic.

"How could you throw those years away if they meant so much to you?" I asked flippantly. I wasn't going to waste perfectly good tears on someone so undeserving. Tears were for things like death…and tax audits. Murder of a relationship certainly wouldn't qualify.

"Baby," he cooed. "It was a cry for help!" He sounded desperate to explain it all away. That was his job. He was well practiced in it. After all, Raleigh was the hub of the state, home to all government offices. There was plenty of use for a defense attorney of even moderate skill.

Emma Nichols

His skills were many…except fucking. He was pretty lousy. Only, I let feelings get in my way. I learned to fake an orgasm that would have made Meg Ryan proud and had Billy Crystal changing his tighty whiteys. At least I wouldn't have to do that anymore.

"Well, Kyle, those cries are falling on deaf ears. I just caught you working overtime at the office on your secretary. Did you find a way to make those billable hours? Damn, I hope so. I hope she's worth it. I hope you two are very happy together…" I just remembered something. "Of course, that could cost you both your jobs…what with that strict fraternization policy and all. Unless you think you can argue that you two weren't spending time together outside of work. I doubt the partners will feel better about that, considering you two probably left a considerable amount of physical evidence on the very table they have their working lunches on." I looked over at Jolie. She smirked and offered me a silent high five.

"So…that's it?" He sounded crestfallen. Clearly, I had managed to crush his pride. I could live with that.

"That's it." I prepared to end the call, but he spoke once more.

"Hey, you have to come get your things. You left some things here. Let me know when you're coming by. We can talk…in person." He had found something to hope for, to hang on to.

I could fix that. "Kyle, it's a toothbrush and some thongs. Keep them.

Wear them if you want. It's the only way you are getting back in my panties again."

After that parting shot, I ended the call. He really couldn't have anything to say after that any way. Taking a moment, I inhaled deeply, waiting for it to fill me, then exhaled slowly. That was one of my relaxation techniques that I had managed to perfect through the years. I reached out a hand to Jolie, she took it and we laughed for a moment.

It only took a moment for her to break the silence. I knew she would. Jolie is predictable like that, couple that with her curiosity and her need to live vicariously through me…I'd be spilling details in no time.

Sure enough, she had turned in her seat; her short brown pixie cut allowed full view of her face. While her hair color was quite ordinary, she had these big green eyes, a tiny button nose, and small full lips that were really great at kissing. Well, they were on that epic trip ten years ago. It had been a while since I could attest to her skill.

Jolie gave my hand a squeeze before releasing it and voicing her thoughts. "So, where are we going? Any plans yet?" She was practically bouncing in her seat.

I smiled at her. That was the question I had been pondering from the start. "I wanted to be able to think and relax and enjoy some sun."

She nodded happily. "The world is our oyster. I brought my passport."

Flipping open my purse beside her, I pulled mine out and said, "Me, too!"

In the end, we decided to go as far away as simply as possible. We drove to a nearby Starbucks to regroup and decide where to go. We were all business working at the table; our laptops had helped us book a cabin on the next Carnival cruise leaving the following afternoon from Charleston, South Carolina. So we were going to sleep in a nice hotel, cuddled together in the king sized bed. We were so exhausted by the time we stopped that we just barely had the energy to strip down before we climbed into bed.

"Panties or completely naked?" Jolie asked, wondering what our dress code was. She smiled at me slyly. Jolie was dying to break in my bi-bone.

As far as I was concerned, our one night of passion ten years ago didn't count. I was drunk and we were experimenting. I enjoyed it, but that wasn't my normal choice. I like penetration. I like feeling a man fill me. There is something so hot about being connected like that…if you have feelings for the guy you are connecting with. I had feelings for Kyle, but after having gone years without an orgasm, if Jolie wanted to take my mind off things, I wouldn't be opposed to it.

I looked at her without saying a word, opting instead to show her. Slowly, I opened my long coat to reveal what I wore underneath. She followed my form from the sexy black mules, all the way up my toned legs to the top of my thigh highs. I heard her gasp when she realized that all I wore with it was a black push up bra and a tiny black cotton thong.

She walked around the bed, her eyes already filled with longing. Once she was in front of me, she peeled off her shirt. I smiled when I realized that she wasn't wearing a bra, but then again, she didn't really need one. Soon she dropped her jeans to reveal her own black cotton thong.

"Oh, look. We match!" I joked. Only…she silenced me with a kiss. It was a greedy kiss, as though the years of pent up sexual tension between us was finally going to erupt.

"Almost," she said, as she kissed her way down my neck. As though she had done this a million times, she reached behind me and unhooked my bra. She slid it down my arms and quickly smiled in satisfaction as my boobs bounced freely. She held them in her hands, a warm sensual look on her face. This time, I knew there would be no excuses for me.

"You know I'm not bi," I said quietly, willing to risk shattering the mood to save our friendship.

"I know," she said simply, "but you *are* curious and that is enough." Then she bent her head and began to suck on one nipple while caressing and flicking the other hard nub.

I could feel myself getting wet and uncomfortable with need. Maybe women really did know how to satisfy other women better. It sure seemed that way at the moment. When she pushed me toward the bed seconds later, I was more than happy to comply.

Soon, she had my panties down and her fingers were working their way inside me. It was that gentle come hither motion that had my g-spot responding. My body was shuddering. For the first time in a really long time, I was crying out in excitement, moaning and writhing.

She pulled her hand back and I sobbed. "No…more," I heard myself beg. That was new. Hell, all of this was new and welcome and so very appreciated. "I need something in me," I pleaded.

"You'll have something in you," Jolie said.

I could tell she felt powerful and in control. Smiling, I let her feel that way. Let her have her moment. That excited her as much as it excited me to have her licking and sucking all around my clit. Then I felt her fingers enter me once more while the licking and sucking continued. It was too much.

Before I knew what I was doing, I had grabbed her head and held her in place, right where I wanted her. Her free hand slid up my flat stomach and found my boob. By now, I was throbbing everywhere. The blessed release that I needed so badly was beginning to take hold. Ah, but I'm not a taker. I give, too. So, I stopped her, released her head and moved until out bodies were parallel.

Soon I was fondling her tits. They were so tiny, such small little nubs. There was just enough nipple for me to wrap my mouth around it and apply pressure. It was so hot getting her all excited.

Really, I had no idea what I was doing. My only advantage was that as a female, I knew what felt good to me. So, I did that to her. I loved having my nipples manipulated and massaged. I loved having my nipples played with licked and sucked. All I did was what I loved having done to me. It worked. How did I know? While I maintained the peace with Kyle all these years by faking orgasms, Jolie didn't believe in that. She believed in letting the person know, in making them work for it.

Only with her, there was no work. It was shared mutual pleasure. I couldn't imagine experiencing this with anyone else. Who else would I feel comfortable enough to open myself up to like this? I had yet to meet that man…or woman.

We were grinding our kitties together. Two shaved naked pussies rubbing until we purred in pleasure. Oh, there was pleasure. We each came…I definitely came twice. I may never be able to thank her enough for ending my drought with a double orgasm.

Finally, we fell asleep, all tangled in each other's arms. There was no way we could stay awake after that. There was no sex marathon. We were completely spent, entirely satisfied. It was just as well; morning and the cruise would come soon enough.

I was halfway through my shower when Jolie decided to join me. While I fully intended to simply shower and get ready for the day, clearly she had other plans. Thankfully, I am flexible…in every way imaginable. Still, considering the time, we had until checkout, I couldn't relax, couldn't get too carried away. This was the beauty of our friendship…Jolie recognized it.

"Worried we're not going to get out of here on time?" She asked after letting my nipple slide out of her mouth.

"You know me. I can't relax," I said casually. "Thank you for last night, though. It was…perfect."

"Well, good. Let me know if you want any perfect moments on the cruise, okay?" She squeezed my ass and hauled me against her lean, wet body.

For the first time in such a long time, everything felt right, like I was headed the right direction, on the right path. We'd have seven uninterrupted days to bond and plan our move. That was what I intended to focus on.

Boarding went so much faster than I expected. We drove through a maze of cones and showed our boarding passes and passports more times than I could count. We had our picture taken.

Then we boarded the ship, went to our room, and dolled up while we decided what to do first. I wanted to hit the bar or the buffet, or both. Jolie had other plans.

"Wait!" She exclaimed. "Look what I brought." Then she pulled a bottle of Chateau Montelena Chardonnay out of her bag. We're wine snobs. We can afford to be. We worked for it. We earned it. We don't apologize for it. We have our own code of rules that we live by. To each his own. This is ours.

That's when we called the steward and asked for glasses and a corkscrew. It made for a lovely moment when we toasted to the future and reminded each other of the rules…no settling and no settling down. Before long, on my empty stomach, I was feeling a nice warm buzz. Jolie announced that she was taking a nap. I countered with an announcement that I was going to need some food or risk a massive headache and serious hangover. That would throw a wrench in our plans.

As I left, she collapsed on the bed, sprawled out, typical Jolie style. I smiled at her, even though she wasn't watching and would never know. For the first time since we left, I could feel myself relax and truly felt happy. It didn't take much.

All over the ship, the party atmosphere had taken hold. The cruise was predominantly made up of adults, thank god. Nothing will ruin a good time faster than a crying baby or whiny toddler. Shoot, throw in a child with a full-blown temper tantrum and I want to put a loaded gun in my mouth. I seem to have managed to escape any hint of maternal instincts. I have yet to experience a biological clock scare. I'm probably more likely to encounter biological warfare on American soil than suffer from that ailment. Who knows? Maybe I'll feel differently in five or ten years. At the same time, I seriously hoped not.

The aromas of the buffet on the lido deck hit me the minute I exited the elevator. Then I remembered that if I planned to enjoy the buffets and maintain my slim size six figure then I would need to start taking the stairs. I frowned. Maybe I should take the mid-morning Pilates class that seemed to be offered daily, or walk the track. I chuckled. I don't own a pair of sneakers. Pilates it would be.

After loading a plate with salad, fruit, potato salad, and some nice southern fried chicken, I found a table for two by the windows that was vacant. Setting the plate down on the granite, I started to pull out my chair when a man came out of nowhere and did it for me. He wasn't in uniform. This wasn't a crew member being helpful. Nope. I had already attracted a new douche. How the hell did they always seem to find me? If this was any indication as to how the rest of the week was going to go, seven days was going to feel like a year. I'm not the kind to hibernate in the cabin to avoid problems. I find a way to make them go away.

This time would be no different. After he helped me push in the seat, I spoke. "Thank you." Then I focused on my food and started eating my salad. Sometimes, I just can't get enough roughage.

"You are welcome, gorgeous." He smiled at me, a smile that clearly cost him more than most people make in six months. "So, do you have a name?"

I was chewing and didn't rush that part to answer him. It would be good for him to wait. He needed to be as uncomfortable as he was making me feel…or would have been making me feel if I wasn't already worn out on men at the moment. Leisurely, I swallowed.

"Yes." Then I loaded my fork with another bite and kept on eating.

Clearly, I had flustered him…not enough for him to leave me alone, mind you, but his soft underbelly was beginning to show. It was all squishy and pink. He laughed it off. "What is it?" He asked in what was probably his most seductive tone.

"You already guessed it. Gorgeous. It's right there on my birth certificate. Imagine how badly that could have gone had I not lived up to the hype." I looked at him evenly, not even cracking a smile.

Would you believe he just kept talking, like we were old friends or soon to be bedroom buddies? That guy couldn't have pried his way into my room with a crow bar. Nope. My vagina was closed to him for sure.

Finally I interrupted him, which was just as well since I had tuned out everything after his empty chuckle. "So, dude, what makes you think I was eating alone?" I asked with more than a hint of annoyance.

"Well, you walked in here alone," he began nervously.

"Yes, well, that's not the same thing as *being* alone." This was the kind of moment that normally Jolie would rescue me from. She would show up and do something to ensure the guy knew we were "lovers." Maybe this time I was on my own. Then I saw him. He had those classic good looks, pretty without looking feminine; a strong jaw, beautiful deep blue eyes, and rich brown hair that was thick and begged to be touched. More importantly, he didn't have a wedding ring. He didn't seem to be meeting anyone. Why couldn't *that guy* have pulled out my chair?

Standing, I stepped in front of him. "Babe, did you not see me? I was right here. Did you get my Coke?" I could see that he was mildly shocked. I could fix that. In a few seconds he was going to be majorly shocked. I planned to render him speechless…and malleable. I stood on my tiptoes and planted a kiss on the tip of his nose. As I imagined, I was offered a hungrier look. That's when I made my move. Slowly, I matched my lips to his and then shifted so that I was angled and we were kissing…really *really* kissing. He played along. Seconds later he had played right into my hand. Wow wow wow.

"Help me, please," I breathed into his ear.

"Anything for you, sexy." He sealed his vow with a kiss on my cheek that totally did not suck. He looked over at my intruder. "Who's this guy?" He asked, jerking his thumb in the guy's direction.

"I have no idea. I'm sure he was just keeping the seat warm for you though." I smiled at him and frowned over at the guy who was keeping me from my meal.

"Uh, yeah, I was just leaving," the man mumbled. Then he stood up as he muttered apologies and soon walked away.

The new guy sat down. I stared over at him. "Hey, don't mind me. I just ended up getting drawn into your little charade. Hope you don't mind if I enjoy my meal while we keep up appearances?" He smiled.

"Nope. We're good," I replied.

Though I was smiling at him, I had little to say. There was so much going on in my mind…and thanks to Jolie, having an orgasm wasn't part of that. Still, I wasn't going to turn down the possibility of some amazing guilt-free sex with a hot guy for anything. Only I wasn't sure how to gain his attention. My smile hadn't worked. The kiss hadn't accomplished anything. What was it going to take to get a man like that to be interested in spending a few meaningless days on a cruise with me? Guess I'd simply have to try the direct approach.

"Are you married?" If that didn't break the ice, nothing would.

"No," he said, cocking his head.

I leaned in. "Really? Because you look like the marrying kind." I took another bite of my potato salad.

Throwing his head back to laugh, he said, "I run too fast. No one can catch me, let alone keep up!"

"Thank you for saving me. I'm here with my friend. She is napping right now. I'm not used to having to fend off guys anymore," I admitted as I kept on eating. Isn't it nice when you don't want anything from someone and you can just be yourself? That was the freedom I felt around Mr. Bedroom Eyes.

He smiled and I saw he started to extend his hand. I knew he was about to introduce himself, so I stopped him. "Listen, you can tell me your name, but I'm just going to forget it. I'm lousy with names."

"Okay, so we're not exchanging names? Is there anything you would like to exchange?" He smirked.

"Yes, as a matter of fact. How about bodily fluids?" I smiled and stared at him with a suggestive look.

He…choked on his Coke. When he finally stopped coughing, I was about finished eating. I don't let much come between my food and me even if I don't look like it.

"Sorry, I'm not used to women being so direct," he said with a smile as he wiped his face.

"I don't play," I said honestly. Then I stood. I am known for my exits. As I turned, giving him full view of what I considered my best feature, I shot over my shoulder, "Think about it." Then I walked away. Always…and I mean *always* leave them wanting more. I didn't have to look back to know that he was staring at me. Let him stare. With my head up and shoulders back, I headed to the elevator.

Chapter 2

When I returned to the room, Jolie was awake and getting ready in the bathroom. Apparently it was time to put on our best face before meeting and greeting the rest of the ship. She walked out wearing a short black sundress.

"Did I miss anything?" She asked with a big smile. I know why she smiled. It seemed like I always had some story to tell. There was always something happening to me, around me, with me. I like my life. Through the years, I have come to discover that life is what you make it. So, I make mine fun and exciting, even unintentionally.

"The usual," I announced. "I was hit on by some skeevy guy, and rescued by a hot one." I smirked.

"Awesome," she said with a laugh. "So, who's the guy and what took you so long?" She joked.

"I don't know." I shrugged.

"No name?" She looked at me suspiciously.

"I told him not to bother. We're on this ship for a week. I'm sure we'll bump into each other once or twice." I smirked as I imagined it.

Jolie laughed. She knows me too well. "Is that the same number of times you expect to be bumping uglies?" She asked.

"Hey, mine is very pretty," I argued playfully. "You should know that after last night."

"Yours is beautiful and sexy," she agreed, walking over to plant a kiss on my cheek. "Let's go. Time to mingle."

"Ugh," I joked, "I hate mingling."

The party atmosphere was contagious. It was difficult to focus on anything. So, we agreed to take the day off. I pulled out my laptop and settled in at the Serenity adult hot tub area on the back of the boat. Jolie headed off on her own to do some exploring. Since the cruise was new to so many people, few had discovered this secret little cozy quiet spot. My lounger was the perfect blend of sun and shade, so that I could get some color, but not risk burning.

I was lying on my belly, searching places to move. There were certain criteria, our move rules. We never lived in the same state twice, so we had to pick our city carefully. We had to move at least 500 miles from the last location. There were states that we had ruled out before we ever visited…like Iowa, and Kansas, even West Virginia. There were states that were ranked higher…since we loved the sun. Currently, the debate was between Charleston, South Carolina; Savannah, Georgia; and Las Vegas, Nevada. In my mind, Vegas was winning. With some research, I could cinch that all up.

"Whoa, I better get those shoulders," a seductive male voice said.

Because I was so engrossed in my research, I didn't pay much attention. Then two strong hands gripped my shoulders, and I could feel warm lotion being rubbed into my skin. Naturally, I jumped. Who the hell would touch some woman he didn't know? I shot up in the seat only to come face to face with Mr. Bedroom Eyes himself. Damn, he was good looking, especially with that playful sparkle in his eyes.

"You?" I asked. "Why?"

"Obviously because I didn't want your shoulders to burn. What kind of husband would I be if I let you get burned?" He wore a playful look on his face.

"A lousy one," I agreed with a smile.

"So, I've been thinking about what you said earlier," he began.

I chuckled. "You must have given it a lot of thought. After all, I haven't seen you for all of an hour."

"As a matter of fact, I have," he smiled. "Will you come walk with me?" He held out a hand to help me gracefully climb off the lounger. I love courteous men; they are such a rare breed.

Taking his hand, I stood and paused a moment to look him in the eye before I gathered my bag and tucked the laptop into it. I liked what I saw in those eyes, no deception, just simple truths and a confidence that spoke volumes without being cocky in the least. Huh. I was apparently better at picking a husband on the fly than I was at selecting a long-term boyfriend.

We walked down the stairs and through the doors into the main atrium of the ship. "Where are we going?" I asked, since we didn't seem to be strolling, but instead walking with both purpose and destination in mind.

"You'll see," he smiled.

We walked further without speaking, my anticipation building. Finally, he broke the silence. "See, I have given both your dilemma and your offer careful consideration. It's clear to me that there is really only one solution." He smiled broadly at his proclamation.

"Oh, really?" I asked with an eyebrow raised. "And just what is my dilemma?"

"Obviously, you need a great protector to fend off unwanted men on this cruise," he announced, puffing out his chest for effect, further proof that he was the protector I needed.

I smiled because he was so damn cute. "Oh, but I have Jolie," I remarked.

"Listen, if this Jolie exists, I have yet to see her. You keep claiming her, but both times we've met, she was nowhere to be found." He shrugged and looked about. "So, I think you should consider my offer. It's a pretty great offer."

"Oh, really. And just what is that?" Looking about, I realized that we had stopped in the cruise ship jewelry shop. Then Mr. Bedroom Eyes dropped to one knee. I backed up a step. "What are you doing?" I asked, confused and concerned. This could go very badly. I may have misjudged him completely.

"Relax," he urged. "I just have one very important question to ask you. And these things are better said with jewelry than I ever could with words."

I started to take a second step back. I'm a runner. Only he grabbed my hand and halted my escape.

"Will you be my wife for the week?" He asked. Then he batted his eyelashes at me.

It really took all the pressure off. Throwing my head back, I let out a huge laugh…a combination of relief and pure joy. "Are you sure you don't want to date me? I hear there's a lot more sex in dating than there is in marriage?"

He stood slowly, contemplating the idea. "This is true, but since I've had no so sex with you thus far, any would be an improvement. Plus, since you already announced me as your husband, I thought this would keep the charade going."

Tilting my head, I considered it. "What exactly would the stipulations be?" I asked curiously. Here he was trying to lure me in with jewelry I didn't need and could very well afford to buy myself. I wasn't one to be swayed that way.

"Well, that fluid exchange we talked about. As your husband, I want to know that I can have you every time I want you, as often as I want you, without fear of headaches or claims of Aunt Flo visiting." He crossed his arms over his chest.

I laughed. "But what if Aunt Flo is visiting?"

He raised an eyebrow. "Is she?"

I shook my head. "No." I looked him in the eye. "So, I get a ring and a protector, you get sex? Is that the agreement?"

"Mostly. I want quality time, too. I want the boring stuff. I want to watch the sunset with you. I want to watch movies, eat dinner, dance, grab drinks. I want naps in the afternoon and to fall asleep holding you at night. I want it all. The whole package." He took my hands in his and gripped them. "What do you think?"

I considered all he suggested. It seemed like a decent deal. "You would make an excellent rebound," I mentioned as I tried to imagine the negative implications. "I'd like to make a few stipulations of my own." I watched him for a reaction.

"Stipulate away. Whatcha got?" He looked at me intently.

"Okay, I'm not out to catch a husband. So, what if we keep it simple. No names. No phone numbers. No emails. Just enjoy the week." I looked at him hopefully.

"That sounds fair, but I better get my fill of you this week, since I'm never going to see you again." He stared me in the eye.

I chuckled. "I hope you can keep up."

Hauling me close, he kissed me just like I loved to be kissed. It was intense and wonderful, full of promise. May he be as good with that tongue everywhere else as he was on my lips. Slowly, he released me and I could feel my mind reeling, new kinds of intoxication taking hold. Soon, I fully intended to get drunk on this man.

Nudging me, with his head, he turned me toward the jewelry counter. There was a man standing beside it holding out a ring. "What do you think?" He asked.

Studying the ring, I nodded. This was probably the most expensive ring they had. I admired how it looked in the box, but even more how it looked as he slid it on my finger. "Wow," I commented.

"This," he began, "is an Ideal Blue diamond. They are rare and beautiful. They have more facets than a typical diamond. And in this setting surrounded by white sparkling diamonds, it really draws attention." He took a breath. "I know I don't even know your name, but in the time that I've spent in your presence, I have been struck by your beauty, your multi-faceted personality, you sparkle and glow. I hope you know how rare and beautiful that is. Be my wife for the week." He smiled calmly; secure in his words and their ability to sway me.

It worked. I was touched. It was better than any real proposal that I could have imagined. Strike that. I don't imagine proposals. It was, however, better than I have ever seen on TV or read in a book.

"Thank you! I love it!" I said honestly. He passed the salesman a black American Express. As soon as the ring was paid for and we left the store, I turned to him. "So…when does the sex start?"

"Patience, beautiful. These things shouldn't be rushed." He said, lifting my chin with one finger so that he could plant a lingering affectionate kiss on my ready lips.

It made me feel all tingly. I love the tingles. Slowly, gradually, I opened my eyes when I realized no other kisses were coming. I raised an eyebrow at him as I said, "You do know that this little seduction scene is wasted on me, right? I mean...here's the ring; I think we've pretty much established that I'm a sure thing." I waited for his response with arms crossed over my chest.

After Jolie started my furnace the other night, I had been pretty much burning up ever since. I had already vowed to never go that long without an orgasm again. This guy was simply killing me. I had to know if he had the skill to back up his game.

"Yes, so I've gathered. And you should know that I am going to do everything I can to make this a memorable and pleasurable week for both of us." He watched as I slowly started to smile, then he drew me close to his chest. "The way I see it, we both need that."

It felt as though my face was going to break, I was smiling so widely. "Absolutely," I agreed. This regrouping was going to be the best one ever.

Then, an hour later, we were deep in an argument. Midway through our heated discussion, he was smiling. "What are you so happy about?" I asked through tight lips.

"Oh, baby, our first fight!" He seemed to so damn pleased with himself that the mood was contagious and I found I was smiling back in spite of myself.

"What were we fighting about anyway?" I asked, completely thrown off balance by his reaction. This man was unlike any I had ever known. Given my history, that could go either way.

"I asked you to move into my cabin. You refused. I pointed out that you were breaking our agreement. You couldn't understand how. I reminded you that I was supposed to be able to have you wherever and whenever I wanted. You thought you should at least be able to rest in peace. I told you I could give you pleasant dreams. You didn't want to leave Jolie. I predicted that she'd understand. Your words were, 'I highly doubt that.' And then I smiled. All caught up now?" He was positively beaming.

I'm pretty sure at that moment; he had never looked more attractive to me. It was all I could do to resist licking him. Seriously. I wanted to taste him all over with my tongue. ALL. OVER. Knowing the timing and location...in the middle of the casino lounge...was terrible, I simply sighed.

"Ah, sounds like you are conceding to me..." He looked so hopeful.

"If you can convince her, I'll stick to the agreement. If not, we renegotiate. Got it?" Crossing my arms over my chest, I looked at him seriously.

Emma Nichols

Slowly, he leaned towards me, eyes intense, and murmured in my ear, "Let's go to your cabin." He nudged me with his nose and as I tilted my head away from him, he burrowed into my neck and began kissing. Instantly, I could feel my heart begin to race, my body was once more on fire, and I was mildly concerned by how quickly he could change my moods and convince me to go against my better judgment.

Still, I nodded numbly and stood. He took my hand and I led him to the cabin I shared with Jolie, conveniently located on the Empress deck, two floors down. We took the elevator alone, which was rare and beautiful. The entire ride, he was whispering beautiful words in my ear about how attractive I was, and what the closeness was doing to him. "You are so beautiful," he began. "I love how soft your skin is. I could just rub my hands all over you all day and never get enough." He sighed happily in my ear. "You have no idea how excited you have me, how excited your presence keeps me. Those beautiful blue eyes…you must be what Viagra is made of." By the time the door opened, he had pressed into my buttocks so that I could feel his erection. I swear if he'd have suggested it, I would have dropped my panties and bent over right there. I'm pretty sure, from the look on his face, he knew it, too.

We walked down the hall at a brisk pace, exchanging smiles and heated looks. Finally, I stopped in front of my cabin door. Of all the times to have to fumble for my card, this was the worst. My frustration was mounting. Then Jolie opened the door.

Smiling, and looking sexy as hell with her hair all messed up, Jolie asked, "Well, what do we have here?"

Chapter 3

For a brief moment, I thought this was going to be one of those dark disappointing moments of my life. Once again, I was reminded to place more faith and trust in Jolie. For the first time, I was able to see the kind of man Mr. Bedroom Eyes was. While I stood just outside the door, frozen, unsure of what to do next, Jolie stepped back to allow us entry and Mr. BE gave me a gentle push to get me moving in the right direction.

Soon, all three of us were in that small confined space with the door closed behind us. For once, I had nothing to say. I was nursing an unspeakable disappointment as my body thrummed with unfulfilled need. There I stood, Jolie in front of me, Mr. BE behind me, wondering what to say or do.

Suddenly, seductively, Mr. BE's arms slid around me. He pressed into me and my eyelids slammed shut while I instinctively bit my lip as I felt his throbbing cock jerking against my butt cheeks. One of his hands moved low along my belly, finally diving down and pressing hard against my pelvic bone. I was so horny that I thought my knees were going to give out. Then his other hand slid along my side until he reached the juncture of my arm and side, so he slid inwards until he was cupping my boob. Oh, the sweet yearning as he manipulated that hard nub.

I forced my eyes open, giving Jolie a pained look, a pleading look. I wanted her to get out, to leave us to this, to let me enjoy the rock hard cock pressing insistently against me. She was fascinated, watching, and waiting. She wasn't taking a hint. It's not like he was being subtle. In frustration, I managed to grunt out her name. "Jolie," I urged.

Instantly she was moved to action. She reached out to me, ran her hands along my shoulders, and pulled the straps of my sundress down my arms until Mr. BE moved his hands and immediately the dress lay in a pool around my ankles. Honestly, I wasn't sure where this was going, but I was in agony and when I get to that place, pretty much anything goes. That was, after all, how Jolie had her way with me the other night.

As porns go, this…was nothing like it. I was the lucky one, the one with two interested parties striving to pleasure her. I had two different hands playing with my boobs. I knew that I was so ridiculously wet. I could feel the ache. It refused to subside. The two of them continued to stoke the fire. While Jolie kissed a trail down the side of my face, I turned my head to allow her access. The minute my head moved, he was there, claiming my lips. Searing me with a heated kiss that left me whimpering. By now, she had found my nipples and was licking and sucking like it was her job. There were hands everywhere, lips all over me kissing and sucking.

Emma Nichols

The second there was a break in contact by Jolie, I pulled her up and dropped her dress in the same fashion she had done to me moments earlier. Then we both went to work on Mr. BE. We worked together to undress him with such finesse that he had to wonder if we had ever done this before. While he seemed reasonably confident, Jolie helped clear the air before we went too crazy.

"Just so you know, I'm strictly a taco girl. I have tried sausage, but it's not for me. So, you can do everything but stick your dick in me. Got it?" She softened the serious tone of her voice with one of her killer smiles.

He nodded. "And just so you know, I would never do anything to you without my wife's permission." He smiled and winked at me.

Part of me wanted to be so greedy. I really did want him all to myself, but curiosity and need were winning out. So far this had been the most sensual and seductive experience of my life and I just wanted it to go on…and on…and on. I looked him in the eyes and melted. He meant it. He really did. There was no pleading in his face, no begging with his eyes. He would have been perfectly content to not touch her at all. Too bad he was my rebound man. He would have made awesome boyfriend material. All I could say to him was, "You heard her rules. We're good. Just…remember who you're married to." I winked at him.

Then he leaned in and kissed me, hugging me close so that every bit of my naked body lined up with his. His warmth transferred to me and any chill that I might have felt while standing there undressed beneath the air conditioning vent was instantly gone. Before I knew what we were doing, somehow, all three of us were on the bed, writhing, naked, and wanting together.

I'm not sure what I liked best, but there were a few positions that just seemed to make everyone happier. For one thing, I noticed that he never kissed her. He touched her boobs and did his best to help her to feel included, but all the real attention was on me. If I had been capable of loving someone else, I might have picked him in that moment. In fact, somewhere along the way, that's what I decided to do. Just live for one week like it was my last. Let my feelings be. Just *be* with him.

At one point, I finally was tired of all the oral play. After Kyle, I never thought I'd say that, but apparently it is possible. I needed Mr. BE in me. I pushed on him to show him what it was I wanted, for him to be on his back. Once he complied, I straddled him. I was wet, so wet that I knew even his large hard cock would slide right in. Because I wanted to savor this more than I had ever savored any sexual experience my entire life, I slowly slid down all the way until I was impaled on him. Never before have I felt so full. I could barely tighten around him. It was almost too much. Then I relaxed into it and started riding him. Jolie took her cue. His head was thrown back in ecstasy, so she straddled his face. For a moment, I worried how he would react. To me, that is such a personal experience. I had allowed very few people oral access, but he began eating her out in such a way that she was moaning.

Soon we were playing with each other's boobs. Not long after, we were all coming. I think I sped the process up. My reaction to having him inside, my frantic hip thrusts as I struggled to end the torment, my moans, and the way so many of my erogenous zones were being pleased all at once. He could feel my excitement and it enhanced his, which in turn caused him to give Jolie the tongue lashing of her life. She was rendered whimpering and quivering on the bed for a bit after. We barely noticed because we were so wrapped up in each other. He was holding me, wrapped himself around me, ordering us to nap after that. I could do nothing but go along with it. My muscles had received an incredible work out. My mind was struggling to process everything that had happened. My heart was still racing like I had run a marathon. This man was such a bad idea.

Jolie dressed quietly and prepared to let herself out of the room. He stopped her. "Hey, Jolie," he called, raising his head off the pillow to look her direction. She stopped and stared without speaking. "Would you mind if I moved your girl into my room for the remainder of the cruise?" His arms tightened around me while he waited for her response.

She dropped her head to one side as she considered his request. "Will you be giving her plenty of orgasms?" She asked openly.

"More than she can handle," he assured her.

"Then…enjoy. I'll collect her again at customs after the cruise." She smiled at me, turned and headed out the cabin door.

"Well, that settles it," he murmured against my cheek. "Looks like you are staying with me."

I sighed. "Somehow, I think this is going to be a horrible idea. Promise not to fall in love with me," I said seriously in a sad quiet voice.

He laughed. "I promise."

"One last thing. Promise you won't make me fall in love with you," I added. I was more afraid of falling in love than anything. For some people, it was heights or snakes or spiders or the number thirteen. I feared love. People did some stupid shit in the name of love. Happened all the time. It made one party or the other believe in a permanence that simply didn't exist. I sure as hell wasn't going to fall prey to that way of thinking. Ever.

He turned my face to his. "I promise," he said quietly and punctuated that claim with a kiss.

Emma Nichols

Just a few hours later, we were headed to his cabin. He marveled over how light I packed. "Really. One bag." He kept shaking his head.

"Of course. I don't need a lot. And what I decide I need, I buy." I shrugged. I wasn't materialistic in the least. The ring he bought me was the nicest piece of jewelry I owned. I had a few necklaces that I had picked up here and there for under $20. I wore some earrings, but none with gemstones or real quality. That wasn't the life I lived.

When you are a digital nomad, there are no office dress codes, no corporate events, no parties or gatherings you need to impress at. In the past, I have worked beside the pool, at a café, in libraries, in hotels. I have worn everything from bikinis to bathrobes. It fit me. I liked it. Even after ten years, I had no desire to change that for anything.

We finally stopped in front of what must be his cabin door as he was currently opening it with his card. I was careful not to look at the card because it had his name on it. While clearly I was all about breaking some rules, that was not going to be one of them. He pushed the door open and stood aside for effect.

Now, Jolie and I had an ocean view room. That was all I needed. I didn't plan on being in the room much. And I sure as hell didn't want to waste money where I didn't have to. That's what husbands are for.

He had a suite. It was one of the top of the line suites…complete with bathtub and big ass balcony. Only, I was not that girl. I wasn't going to run squealing into the room. I was not going to give him that kind of satisfaction as to impress that easily.

Casually, I entered the room, barely glanced around, and simply lay on the bed seductively. "What now, handsome husband?" I asked playfully.

"Now we refuel. Let's get ready to eat. Fine dining tonight. I'm guessing you don't have anything to wear." He glanced at his watch. It was just 5pm. "Let's go shopping. After that, we'll shower and then go to dinner. Sound good?"

Shrugging, I replied, "Sure, why not?"

Nothing in my life has prepared me for this man. Nothing. Not my bastard of a step-father, not my grandparents' minister, nothing. There is no male in my life to which I can compare this man. Instead of feeling confident and in control like I had been when I contemplated this and even initiated the conversation, I felt like I was waiting for the shoe to drop. I was waiting for him to show his true colors. No one could be that giving, that generous, or that good. Though I had just hours before made the claim that I was going to just *be* this week, I soon found myself just watching and waiting for him to fuck up. They always do. That's what all the men in my life have taught me. They have taught me that men fuck up and when they do, they tend to fuck over the women who love them. These rules I live by, they weren't created out of a passing fancy. No, years of experiment and experience went into their creation.

Now, Mr. BE is here. For the moment. He's spoiling the hell out of me, even though I could well spoil the hell out of myself. I'm so confused. Thank god our first encounter was with Jolie present. I'm going to need back up on this one, but first, a shower.

Without thinking, I automatically followed my normal routine, gathering my clothes and toiletries, I headed into the bathroom to shower and get ready for the night. For some reason, it felt really important to me that he be impressed with my efforts, this nameless husband I had acquired over the last few hours. So, when I was in the shower and he suddenly walked in and pulled back the curtain, I reacted. "Hey! No peeking," I said as I covered as much skin as possible with my arms and crossed legs.

"To peek would suggest that I'm not supposed to look," he said in a low voice. "I, however, am able to look wherever and whenever I want." With that proclamation, he leaned in and kissed me on the center of my forehead, on each temple, on the tip of my nose, then hovered over my lips, until ours were not even a breath apart. I was instantly ready for him, but he said, "Later." Then he stood straight and walked back out of the bathroom.

It took me a moment to recover from his closeness. It took me longer than that to process what had happened. I'm pretty confident the man was trying to seduce me. Damn if it didn't work. How was I going to survive four courses in the dining room? I thought for a moment, then a smile spread across my face. I would simply have to enjoy torturing him, too.

Thus began our game of cat and cat. No one wanted to be the mouse. Instead, we suddenly viewed each other as prey. Ah, a pretend marriage of real equals. Immediately, I reconsidered my dress for the meal. I certainly wasn't at a loss for options. Even though the ship had a limited selection, he bought me...everything they had in my size. Now there were dresses of varying lengths and styles in amazing fabrics and gorgeous colors. Thank goodness the shop hooked me up with a garment bag or I have no idea how I would have managed to get it all back to Raleigh. In the end, I chose something that was tight fitting and showed my boobs to perfection in scarlet. If I was on fire, I was going to look the part. Even more importantly, if I was suffering, I was going to make sure he suffered, too. I wore the tiniest panties I owned, a thong that really consisted of the tiniest cotton patch and three pieces of dental floss that connected with a silver shamrock at the back. They were sexy and suggestive and utterly perfect for this scenario. This time I wore no bra, just some pasties over the nipples to keep it family friendly.

Emma Nichols

As a final touch I sprayed on J'adore perfume in the cleavage, behind the neck, around the throat and in the bend of my arms and behind my knees. Carefully, I applied my smoky eyes, finished with a thick coat of mascara, and completed the look with a rich lush lipstick. I couldn't wait to see his reaction.

Throwing my shoulders back confidently, I walked out of the room in scarlet-strapped heels. Though I tried to behave as if the entire quality of our evening was not based on his first words, to me…they kind of were. I grabbed my clutch, made sure to pack a lip gloss, and my cards, then went to stand near the door. "Ready?" I asked, striking a pose that I hoped would look natural.

He smiled. "Nope. You're not. Not yet." He stood and walked over to me. Then he handed me a jewelry box. I just stared at it in my hands. "Open it," he suggested in a low voice.

After another slight hesitation, I pushed back the lid and discovered a pair of diamond earrings. "So, are these on loan?" I asked, always practical.

"Nope, they are yours. I told you. I want you to always remember this." Then he reached out and affixed one earring to each ear. "I have to admit, it gives me a lot of pleasure to see them on you."

"Know what else can give you a lot of pleasure?" I asked playfully.

He smirked as he looked at me and responded simply, "What?"

Leaning in, I kissed his lips. Growing bolder, I kissed a trail up his jawline until I reached his ear. After nipping at the lobe, I murmured, "Me." Then I broke contact and headed for the door. Always, and I can't stress this enough, *always* leave them wanting more. I turned as I reached for the handle. "Coming?" I asked.

That snapped him out of his reverie. Soon he was trailing after me, which was precisely the effect I had hoped for. We walked to the elevator, punched the button, and as we waited, his hand found the small of my back. I loved that. So few men still do that, lay a hand on a woman's lower back, but they totally should. It is such a protective and loving gesture. So why was Mr. BE doing it?

I glanced up at him quizzically. He smiled and responded, "What? You don't want your husband to touch you? That would break our agreement." He winked at me. Just then the doors opened and we headed down to dinner.

Clearly he knew. He knew what so few men had figured out. I was definitely pulling out all the stops at dinner. As soon as we were seated, my hand found his upper thigh. He jumped the first time I squeezed it and started massaging it. His eyebrows rose, then he calmed down, relaxed into and upped the ante. Soon, he had one hand knotted in my hair, playing with it, massaging my neck, and rubbing my scalp. If I wasn't careful, I'd have my face in his lap before dessert. Damn, this man was simply not playing fair.

As the meal wore on, I could tell we were both affected by the other's actions. We excused ourselves before coffee. He claimed he had the ulcer. I claimed I didn't want to be up half the night. His eyebrows rose and I knew what he was thinking. More than anything, I hoped he meant what he suggested. I really wouldn't mind being kept up half the night for this. After all, tomorrow was a full day at sea before we even reached Grand Turk. I didn't mind missing breakfast, especially when there was 24-hour room service. Hell, at the moment, I wouldn't mind if we never left the cabin.

We walked to the elevator and Mr. BE looked at me seriously. "So, did you want to get a drink, or take a walk?"

Oh, he was good. Well, I wasn't going to be the one to break first. "You know what? I think I'd like to do both," I responded calmly as I hooked my arm through his. *That's right, Alysin,* I thought, *play it cool. You've got this, girl.* Only, I didn't. I was jelly and hot and quivery inside. I tingled in places that had never tingled before. Worse, there was this strange stirring like something in me long dormant had been awakened. *Keep it together.*

We walked to the piano bar where he ordered us a bottle of wine. Not a glass. Not a carafe. No, we were having an entire bottle. It was some

Pinot Noir that he claimed I would really enjoy. "I don't know about that," I joked. "I like my wine sweet."

He reached over grabbed my left hand that bore his ring and kissed it. "Just like you like your men?" He asked with a smile.

"Oh, no. Past experience tells me I like my men dry and nutty." I slowly pulled my hand back as I smiled happily at him. "How do you like your women?"

"Hmmm," he said while scrunching his face up into what was apparently his thinking look. "I haven't found any women that I've liked in a long time. No attraction. No compatibility. They sounded perfect for your men...very nutty."

I laughed, but I couldn't help but wonder how long it would take for me to regret that Mr. BE was my rebound. Every minute that I knew him, I liked him more. In relationships, that seemed to be half the battle. Shoot, I didn't even want Kyle around half the time. No wonder I kept turning him down when he asked about us living together. It's good that we're not together. It's simply lousy the way it ended. In my mind, Kyle will forever be branded a coward.

Somehow, when I was finally present once more, done with the reminiscing about the state of my life, I realized that he had his arm around me. Moments later he was whispering in my ear, "Dance with me."

Emma Nichols

I glanced about the room. "No one is dancing," I said. "I don't even think the room is big enough to dance."

"Ha," he said seriously. "Just follow my lead."

Raising an eyebrow I responded in the sexiest voice I could manage, "Don't I always?"

He chuckled. "It's a little early on in the relationship for me to comment on that, but if you're keeping track…so far, so good." Then he yanked me off my seat and into his arms. Next thing I knew, we're swaying to the music, our bodies pressed together so tightly that I couldn't figure out where one of us began and the other one ended.

The entire seduction scene was taking a toll on me. There was entirely too much touching, too much closeness. There were entirely too many clothes and people. It made me feel things I neither wanted nor had any business feeling. Yet…I couldn't stop. The whole time, there was also this underlying need to find out what would happen next. I had to ride this out, let it run its course. So what if I lost myself for a week? That was all I was capable of at the moment. I had no idea where I was going to move. Starting something was not an option.

As we spun around together, I was so lost in the moment that I never realized how many people were actually paying attention to us, watching our every move, until the song ended. Then…he dipped me. I've seen it in movies. It always looked so fun, so effortless, and with

Mr. BE…it was. Damn, that man and his amazing upper body strength. My hair brushed the floor. I threw my head back like I had seen on screen, and then he pulled me up and against him.

"You look flushed," he said as he nuzzled my neck and walked me back to our wine.

By now we had each had a glass of the wine to drink. Add to that the drink with dinner, the dancing, and the non-stop foreplay…yeah, I'm sure I was flushed. "I am hot…and bothered," I said, while watching him for a reaction.

His face was buried in my hair at the moment. "Not bothered, too," he murmured against my ear. I didn't have to speak; I merely nodded. "Well, let's go then." He pulled away long enough for me to feel the absence.

It surprised me, but not as much as his next move. Picking up both wine glasses, he passed one to me. Then, doing that hand on my lower back thing that I was already craving, we headed out of the piano bar and up to the lido deck. All I could think was…*wrong direction!* I wanted to be naked, in his arms, in our cabin. Crap! I was using words like 'ours' already. His. His cabin. Mr. BE's cabin. Dammit.

We headed through the automatic doors and that ridiculous blower as we exited onto the top open-air deck of the boat. It was dark, the kind of dark it should be out in the middle of the ocean. The only lighting was the ship's party lights strung around the top. He walked me to the back of the boat, through the buffet, pausing briefly to pick up a few things…some strawberries in a bowl…some whipped cream, a bit of chocolate sauce. I loved the way he thought, as long as he was thinking what I was thinking. Damn, I hope he was thinking what I was thinking.

His little snack screamed 'fun with food.' It was something I had always enjoyed, with the right guy. With the wrong guy, it really wasn't worth the mess. Oh, but something about Mr. BE told me that I was going to enjoy every moment with him.

When we reached the back of the ship, I realized that we were alone. It had to be later than I thought. That's what happens when I'm having fun. Time flies. Suddenly, my chest tightened. This week…would fly and then it would be over. I closed my eyes. Just enjoy this. Just make some memories. Fuck. I was turning into a regular girl after one day with my mystery man.

"Would you like to sit down?" He asked.

Really. I didn't. Sitting suggested a need for comfort because we were going to be there for a while. I wanted to be alone with him while struggling to play it cool. Suddenly, this had turned into a power struggle. And I played to win. "Sure," I said as I sat down in a seat that was far away from the door, right up against the railing. If we couldn't actually be alone, I was at least going to feel like we were.

Once seated, I propped my feet up on the railing. I knew that it would make the dress fall just right, exposing my legs. I had always been told that they had been one of my best features. I tone up with regular yoga, eat right, and have never been pregnant. I have plenty of good features. I'm not perfect, but I like me. I'm comfortable naked. I'm especially comfortable naked with him.

A smile spread across his face as he glanced at my legs. Pushing the dish toward me, he asked, "Care for a snack?

"Do I get to be dessert?" I asked leaning my upper body on the table. It has always served me well to plant ideas in men's minds. If I knew men, he would be imagining sex with me…right now.

To up the ante, I picked up the reddest, lushest strawberry I set eyes on then dipped it in whipped cream. Slowly, I guided it to my open waiting mouth, taking a moment to lick the whipped cream first. I closed my eyes as I bit into it and pretended to be savoring that bite way more than I actually was. When I opened my eyes once more, he was smiling.

On his extended finger, a healthy dollop of whipped cream. "Oops," he said.

"Funny, you don't look like you made a mistake," I murmured as I reached out, wrapped my hand around his, and drew it to my mouth. In seconds, I had licked the cream off his phalange with a combination of short flicks and long lingering licks. "Well, it looks clean," I began, "but just to be sure…" Then I took his finger in my mouth, his whole finger, while staring into his eyes. I sucked on it a moment, letting it slide out then back in as I relished the feel of his fingerprint on my tongue. I swear I felt him shiver. Finally, I took it out and said, "All better."

Now he was clean, but, if I had done it right, his mind was dirty. With any luck, filthy dirty. How I wanted this man. I loved it and hated it. Still, I wanted this man.

Gazing up at him from under my eyelashes, he surprised me by suddenly cupping my face and drawing me nearer. His kisses were no longer a surprise. I knew his tells. I was definitely about to be kissed.

Mr. BE does not disappoint. Or, rather, he hadn't yet. He has this amazing ability to keep me interested. That was quite the skill in and of itself. He was the perfect combination of attractive and intelligent. He was…dangerous. He was mine…for the week.

Chapter 4

Day two of the cruise dawned sunny and bright. Still, I woke long before Mr. BE. I wasn't sure what to do with myself. Knowing nothing about his habits, I decided to order some room service and shower while I waited. It was pretty perfect. Really it was. I felt so…relaxed as I sat on the balcony in my bathrobe, sipping my Earl Grey, snacking on my fruit salad, looking out over blue water as far as the eye could see, while reminiscing about the night before. No wonder the poor guy was tired out.

Let's face it our hormones were working overtime all night. Somehow, I finally wore him down. I managed to convince him to come back to the cabin. After the whipped cream, our evening only grew steamier and that's why we ended up continuing our night of fun with food on our own balcony.

There was something about the way the stars looked on that black velvet sky. There was something about the way the strawberries and whipped cream tasted when it was fed to me by him or licked from his fingers. Before long, I had convinced him to lie on the bed. He was reluctant. He worried I was too eager, worried I would rush things that we had all the time in the world for…if you considered a few days all the time in the world.

Emma Nichols

Finally, I pulled out my camera from the bag. I carry it with me everywhere. It is the lifeblood of my business. Though I was never professionally trained, in the digital world, I am considered a very talented photographer. I capture people and places with my eye for beauty. Then I sell them to magazines. Those that don't sell right away for a specific purpose are then uploaded and sold on sites that offered royalty free images. I have an extensive portfolio from years of work. My income…grows and grows. My overhead is non-existent. I travel as much as I want whenever I want. I make money going for walks. While I had planned to mostly take this trip off and focus on the next move, this was a welcome wrench in the plans. So when he balked and worried we weren't savoring the moment, I started taking pictures.

"How will I get copies?" He asked. "No names, no phone numbers, no emails…no pictures." He frowned then recovered and had a twinkle in his eye.

Sure, for a moment I rather hoped he had decided that we would break our agreement. Sure, there was that instant that I was ready to tattoo my name and contact information on the inside of his arm so that he would never lose it. Only, that wasn't what he suggested.

"What if we get some of the pictures printed on the trip?" He asked. "We could leave with a concrete version of our memories…"

His idea had merit, but I wasn't entirely convinced that we would be able to master the execution. Did I want to spend an excursion trying to find a one-hour photo place? Did I want to waste a minute that we could be spending making memories by trying to preserve them on film?

"What if I give you the SD card before we get off the boat?" I asked, practically.

He nodded. "That would be great, but what about you?"

"What about me?" I asked, my teeth already grazing his neck as I pointed and shot. Yeah, I may have done this once or twice. I have modeled in my photos. Who knows better than me what I want the pictures to look like? That's right. No one.

"Don't you want some pictures, too?" He asked. He had sounded almost hurt even as I distracted him with my tongue.

"Oh, don't worry, I also travel with my laptop. I'll download the pics and then give you the SD card." I really just wanted to get back to where we left off. I ran my free hand down his washboard abs. He had just a dusting of hair down the middle of his chest. Happily, I followed the trail down into his boxer briefs.

Once again, his cock sprang out at me. I had never grown so used to another man's presence so quickly…ever. Mr. BE was easy to be with.

Emma Nichols

He was the kind of guy who would be easy to fall in love with. He was the most dangerous man ever. I've had the tattooed bad boys. I liked them. I enjoyed them. They were fun…and temporary. What I had never had, never done, was enjoy a straight-laced good guy. This guy was hard to figure out. There were no tattoos, but not every bad boy wore them like a badge of honor. I was baffled.

That's the trouble with no names, never exchanging personal information. What did I look like…The Mentalist…an FBI profiler? I couldn't figure him out. So I tried to tell myself that it was the mystery of it all making the situation so hot, knowing that we could both be whoever we wanted to be.

At the moment, I was being the chick sucking his dick. It was no easy task. He was hung. Believe it or not, that kind of annoyed me. He shouldn't be so frickin' perfect. He shouldn't be hot and generous and hung. It was so…wrong. He hadn't called me any names. He hadn't made me feel like I was less than I was. He held doors open, unless they were automatic. He pulled out chairs…unless they were attached. Now, I was truly studying him, getting to enjoy him on my terms, alone, without Jolie, and I had to admit he had one of the prettiest dicks I'd ever been laid with.

It didn't take long for me to give up on the blow job. He seemed to be fine with the idea. He, too, was urging me up, hauling me closer to his waiting mouth. Insisting on kissing me with a passion that I had yet to previously experience. Our foreheads were together as we panted some. He was guiding my hips down onto him. Slowly, ever so slowly, he entered me once more.

Just as before, I was insanely ready for him. How could I not be? Oh, but when I opened my eyes I realized how much trouble I was in. He was doing a fine job penetrating my body with his cock, but now he was piercing my heart with those eyes, those gorgeous blue bedroom eyes. I was almost embarrassed by how quickly that first orgasm arrived. Remember how I opened my eyes? Yeah. Then. While, he felt amazing inside me and he was doing a phenomenal job working those nipples with his hands…it's what his eyes did to me that truly sent me over the edge. Damn.

He knew it, too. He knew when I came, when my breath caught and my body shuddered inside. He felt me trying to ride out that orgasm, letting wave after wave take me far away. Though I've never been one to speak during sex, clearly he was.

"Come back to me, baby," he murmured against my lips. "Come on."

Part of me was spent. Part of me wanted to keep going forever. So we continued for as long as we both could stand it. Hours of foreplay. Hours of him in me. Multiple orgasms for both of us.

Now…he slept…when I wanted nothing more than for him to be awake. Would you believe that it wasn't for sex? Nope. I wanted to talk. This guy was killing me.

It was close to noon when he finally woke. He looked rested, and happy, and surprised. I had heard him rustling around in bed, the kind of sound that normally precedes someone waking up. I was right. He was. When I finally closed the laptop, stood, turned, and walked back in from the balcony, he was laying on his side smiling at me.

"What are you doing here?" He asked happily.

I looked at him sideways, unsure of what he was asking. Had he forgotten me already? Had yesterday meant nothing to him? Luckily, while I was still finding my words, he spoke once more.

"You let me sleep in and then when I woke up, you were still here? I expected you'd be up on the lido deck getting some sun or wandering the ship getting hit on by some strange guy?" He lifted the bedding, welcoming me to join him.

Dropping my bathrobe to reveal that I was au natural underneath, I climbed in not really knowing what to expect. "As your wife, I figured I should be here for you when you woke. Here am I. Ready to meet your needs. Do you have any unfulfilled needs?" I asked playfully as I snuggled against his warm naked body.

Already, I knew that he had morning wood. Funny name…morning wood. It should just be called 'waking wood.' Experience had taught me that guys could get it any time of the day with sleep. His wood was really lunch wood or early afternoon wood. He rubbed it against me and I was convinced it was about to become my wood once more. I smiled suggestively.

"I may have one need that you could fulfill if you'd like," he said.

"Anything," I responded. Oh, and I meant it. A week was not going to be long enough.

"Coffee. Can you call for room service? After a coffee and a shower, I'll be ready to go to lunch…unless you just want to order in?" He smiled at me.

Oh, how I wanted to order in. Then I shook my head. Talk. We needed to talk. "God, do you have to be so…distracting?" I asked.

He looked at me taken aback. "What do you mean?"

"While you were sleeping, I had this whole talk planned in my head that we needed to have. Then the minute you wake up, it's all but forgotten because you are so hot!" I frowned at him.

"Wow. I've never felt the need to apologize after being complimented before." He smiled. "So do I say 'thank you' or 'I'm sorry?' Honestly, I'm not sure where to go with this."

"Apology accepted," I said as I laid my head on his chest. Instantly, his beating heart, the feel of his skin against my cheek, and the scent of him mesmerized me.

"Sooooo, the talk? Did you fill in my lines in your head or did you want me to actually participate?" He chuckled as he ran a hand up and down my side.

"Oh, yeah." I sat straight up because this was not going to work with us snuggled together in bed. Then, I left the bed entirely, grabbed my robe, and sat down after I cinched it around my waist. "Whew. There."

He frowned. I was making him nervous. In the past, I would have relished that, the control of it. Now, I wanted to comfort him. "Listen, you are very distracting. I need space."

"Okay?" He sat up fully in bed.

"We didn't talk about this, and it was really irresponsible of me. I guess I should have mentioned it before." I sighed and decided to dive right in. These talks are better when treated like Bandaid removal. "So, we haven't been using protection."

"Oh, that!" He said and laughed. "Don't worry. It's safe." He waved his hand and stood to head to the bathroom. "I thought you wanted to talk about something serious."

I stood and followed him. "This is serious. I don't want to walk away with a souvenir from this trip," I said in an irritated voice. "I don't think you understand the gravity of the situation."

He had just finished peeing. He turned and looked at me. "Listen, babe, I had a procedure. I can't get you pregnant. And I am clean. No transmittable diseases. I'm going to take a shower. Can you order my coffee?" With that, the conversation was over…apparently. He had already tuned me out and started messing with the water temperature.

A thought occurred to me. "Aren't you worried that I have something? Look how quickly I fell into bed with you? I could have herpes…the gift that keeps on giving. I could have The HIV! I could kill you!"

He whipped around. "Babe, *you* won't be killing me. For the love of God, coffee, please!" With that, he stepped in the shower.

While I should have been comforted, I wasn't. The very least I could do was order him coffee, like a good wife. Yes, coffee would be waiting when he finished. So would I.

Sometimes, I wondered if they pulled the guys aside in school. You know, when the girls watch that special movie and talk about getting their periods, what are the boys doing? I've always had my suspicions. Now, I've convinced they have a workshop on being evasive. They are all the same. I tried to talk more. He avoided my questions.

"Listen, if having me wear a condom makes you feel better, then get some. I'll wear them. Otherwise, stop being a nagging wife, drop that line of questioning, and let's enjoy the rest of this week." He was serious. I had hit a nerve. By the looks of it…all of them. Still, if that was as bad as he could get, I could handle this.

Nagging wife. I really had turned all girl. Well…crap.

"Okay then. Let's get lunch and decide how to spend the rest of the day," I said. I went and stood by the door. I could feel him holding back. As much as I wanted to know, we had a week. This wasn't forever. This was the best shot at for now I had. I needed to take it.

We were sitting there talking on the lido deck, listening to music and enjoying the perfect weather…and I mean perfect: cloudless blue sky, gentle cooling breeze, and sun that didn't seem to scorch the minute we were exposed to it. He had eaten a healthy meal…grilled lemon chicken, a mixed greens salad with a side of fruit salad, and now he was scarfing down his second soft serve chocolate ice cream cone. I was fascinated. There was literally not an ounce of fat on him. He had a strong medium build, the kind that looks natural, a product of his lifestyle instead of long hours at the gym. Those are my favorite kind.

I don't believe in being with anyone who is higher maintenance than I am. As chicks go, I am low maintenance.

Standing suddenly, I laughed when I saw him heading back to the ice cream. "Where do you put it?" I asked.

"Well," he said seductively, leaning in to graze my lips with his, "I am planning on working it off…soon. I look at this more as refueling. You have given me quite the workout." Then he kissed my head and walked toward the machine.

Less than thirty seconds later, Jolie came over and sat down. "Where have you been hiding?" She asked with a chuckle.

Leaning back in my seat, the picture of calm, I gave her my most relaxed smiles. "In bed." She raised her eyebrows and smiled. "That's right. We stayed up half the night and slept in to recuperate. It's only a week. We have to make the most of it." I shrugged. Naturally, Jolie saw through me.

"Ut oh," she said. "I thought this guy was your rebound?"

"He is," I protested. "We're sticking to the rules…no names, no contact info. We're just…having a good time. You know me." I looked her in the eye. I tried to give her my most convincing look. It didn't work. On either of us.

"You haven't looked like this since high school, since before we started this life, these rules, and made this plan. It's worked really well for us so far, Alysin Nixon…my little Sin the Vixen. Ten years was a good run. Maybe we should finally make one last move. Maybe you should let him in," she urged.

Glancing over at the ice cream machine, I watched him for a moment. He was happiness and hope all wrapped up in one beautiful manly package. From the looks of it, he had made his ice cream cone and now he was making cone after cone for a line up of kids. They were in the camp on the boat. He looked up and saw me watching him. He smiled and shrugged, completely without guile. I smiled back, even though I was suddenly assaulted with an image of him doing the same thing for a little girl that looked remarkably like I did when I was four. I shook my head.

"No. This is just fun. This is to forget what's his name," I said seriously.

Jolie laughed at me. "Well then you should stop now."

"Why's that?" I asked confused.

"Because clearly you have already forgotten Kyle. Now you are going to be haunted by this guy…a nameless meaningful man." She stood, leaned over and gave me a quick hug. "I promised this chick I'd meet her for a drink. I'll see you later."

Then she walked away. I was left with more to consider, more to think about that I didn't want to. He'd better come back soon. I didn't plan to think much on this trip past where we were going to move when we returned.

At 4pm, we found ourselves wandering through the art gallery. He was getting everything he wished for…there were plenty of boring things to do on the trip. He was the master of the mundane. It wasn't that I didn't like art galleries. I loved them. Once, in high school, I had taken a trip abroad. It was a ten-day tour of France, Italy, and everything in between. (That would be Monaco and Monte Carlo, for those of you who have never had the pleasure of traveling abroad.)

On that trip, I discovered a love of museums that I had never had previously. With my passion for culture, it shouldn't have been a surprise. At the Louvre, the beauty of the Venus de Milo, and the Mona Lisa struck me, but even more…I fell in love with some of the more obscure paintings that were on the walls. There was one in particular. I can't remember the name, but in the background, high up on a hill was a dark and eerie estate. In the foreground, there was a young woman, tied up, drowned in the lake. I stood there and studied it for far longer than I did any other painting. It was huge, the biggest painting I had ever seen. Years later I think of it still, just as I remember visiting the Sistine Chapel and how surreal it was to be wandering around this vast open room, bumping into strangers because we were all too busy looking up to notice those around us.

Emma Nichols

By the time we reached Florence, I had a boyfriend for the trip. He was from another high school that had been paired with ours and had been watching me. I knew it. I felt it all the time. Finally, we spoke. I didn't feel for him. It was just…more fun having someone to share the experience with. More than that, it was a learning experience, one that I repeated time and again. I loved to travel. Soon, my travel boyfriends were my favorite. That first time in Italy taught me much…like boundaries.

By the plane ride home, we arranged to sit together. The flight was long, but it didn't seem that way because…I very nearly joined the mile high club. It's amazing how far you can get under a shared blanket during a movie on a darkened plane. Oh, and he had his hand down my shorts, behind my panties, and his fingers inside me. It was heavenly. I still remember it fondly. More importantly, I learned not to share contact information. Sure enough, within days of returning home, I was getting mail…desperate, lonely, mail…from him. We didn't even have licenses yet and we lived four states apart. Nothing was ever going to come of it. It was fun while it lasted. The experience helped hone my personal philosophy.

No matter what Jolie suggested, I wasn't going to change that philosophy now. Given how this cruise was shaping up so far, I probably would be the one sending the desperate and pathetic emails. Somehow I had to remember that this was just meant to be fun while it lasted.

These were just some of the thoughts rushing through my mind as I stood and stared at the paintings in the ship's art gallery. I had stopped to stare at one painting in particular. It reminded me of Italy, the Mediterranean in particular. There was a stone patio overlooking the blue water. I have a thing for paintings I want to live in. This one…was perfect. I could completely picture sitting at the little bistro table with a glass of wine, watching the sunset.

My reverie was interrupted by a whisper in my ear. "Wow, that one is amazing. Great eye. My favorite paintings are ones that I would love to live in. It makes me think of Italy." He sighed right next to my ear and it made me shiver. Naturally he noticed.

Wrapping his arms around me, he spoke to me once more. "Babe, are you cold? We can't have that," he said lovingly as he ran his hands up and down my arms.

That brought on more chills. Many more chills until finally I had to whip around and look at him. "Stop," I said through gritted teeth. "You are so not helping here."

He paused, leaving his hands on my upper arms. "Oh, would a hug be better?" Then he hauled me against his body.

Surprisingly enough, it did help some. It soothed me in a way that the arm rubs didn't. Then he had to go ruin it.

"Have I told you how sexy you look when you stand there and study art?" He murmured in my ear, tickling me all the way through.

Without thinking, I grabbed his head and stared into his eyes for all of a heartbeat before I slammed my lips into his. There was no way I could get him close enough. No way. Ah, but I had to try.

His lips were just as greedy as mine. We kept it PG for the gallery crowd, but I still heard one older woman mumble, "Must be newlyweds."

I pulled back to smile at her, but he still had his face pressed against my temple. "Oh, we are," I said silkily. "Is it that obvious?" I winked at her. She smiled and walked away.

"You've been staring at this for a good fifteen minutes," Mr. BE said as soon as we were alone again. "I'm going to buy it for you." He kissed my temple before he started to walk toward the woman running the gallery.

I was in heaven. I didn't need this painting any more than I needed the jewelry. It wasn't because I was some gold digger, but there was something really special about being pampered like this, something really great about all these outward signs that he thought of me, cared about me, and wanted to please me. After that time in bed, I didn't have any doubts.

I stepped back as a young man with gloves on came over to remove the painting from the wall. He nodded at me as he carried it into a room to the side no doubt to wrap it and deliver it later to our stateroom. Soon, Mr. BE was shaking hands with the woman and walking back to me.

"Want to go back to the cabin?" He asked with a smile.

Shaking my head, I responded, "We don't need to rush this. We have plenty of time." Then I turned and headed out of the gallery toward the casino. When I had taken several steps and he hadn't caught up to me, I turned and smiled. "Coming?"

He had that look. He knew. I was doing this on purpose. For a moment, I had let my guard down; I had forgotten our deal. Now I was back on track. I said that I would be ready, willing, and amenable to his advances, but I didn't say I was going to bend to his every whim. As much as he had put me off yesterday, I would make him work for it today.

The stunned look had worn off his face, as he stepped up to walk with me, he grabbed my hand, pulled it to his mouth, and said simply, "Touché."

Honestly, I was patting myself on the back…and mostly wishing that I were alone. I would be rubbing myself elsewhere. This man sure did know how to excite me. Now, to prove how strong I was, how unaffected, I had effectively forced myself to suffer. I sighed.

"What's wrong, babe?" He asked with interest.

"I forgot something in the cabin. Want to pick us a lucky table at the casino and I'll be right back." Then I scampered off before his too wise eyes had the chance to figure out what was really going on with me. He didn't call after me. I didn't dare turn to see his reaction. I was practically in a jog to make it back to the room.

Shoving my card in the door, I opened the cabin. The bed had been made. The room looked perfect, all pristine. Without hesitation, I let the straps slide down my shoulders, so that my bare boobs were exposed. There was no time to waste. I had to hurry. If I was going to survive until bedtime, I had to do this.

Climbing onto the bed, I lay on my back and slid my thong out of the way. With one hand, I began manipulating my nipple, first rubbing it with my open palm, and then tugging at the hardened nub. I could feel the excitement building. This wouldn't take long at all. My other hand knew just where to rub around my clit. It felt so amazing so quickly. I was so excited from all the amazing sex that I didn't have to even imagine anything in particular, just feeling what was happening sufficed.

That's when I heard the card in the door, but I refused to stop when I was this close. The lack of knock prior to the card told me it was he.

Let him see me masturbating. I was actually eager to find out how he might respond to the situation.

As soon as he realized what I was doing, he dropped his shorts and yanked down his boxers. He had a hand on his cock and was stroking it as he came closer. Then he dropped to his knees, roughly moved my hand out of the way and buried his face in my soft shaved folds. I gasped when I felt his tongue licking, his teeth nipping, and the sucking gently had me moaning. My hips arched to allow him better access. It was too much, especially, when I heard the sound of him stroking fast and furious. Soon, I was shuddering and quaking. The best part was that he knew I was having an orgasm. I didn't need to grab his head and hold him in place; instead he kept going and let me ride it out. Damn, this man was dangerous.

Slowly, I opened my eyes to check his progress. He was close. There was a healthy amount of pre cum dribbling out the end of his dick. His breathing had changed, ragged and catching. Sliding off the bed, I dropped to my knees in front of him.

"Lay back," I commanded.

Without hesitation, he complied. I moved his hand away from his raging erection. Originally, I intended to take him in my mouth. I was going to let him finish. I was even going to swallow. I was going to be that giving, that memorable…only lately I have wanted to be so selfish. Instead, I climbed on. I straddled him.

His eyes flew open for a moment, and then he let out this guttural groan as I slid onto him. It was incredible feeling him slide into me once more. It was so welcome, so pleasurable…such a perfect fit. My hips found their rhythm. Soon, his hips were meeting mine. We were going at it fiercely, wildly. I couldn't get enough of him. Somehow, without losing pace, he flipped me over onto my back, had me bent nearly in two. Thank God I do yoga. Even then…I wanted more. After being a one trick pony for so long, after years of vanilla sex with that lawyer guy…this man, our chance meeting had changed everything.

I cried out. I couldn't help it. It was so…intense. Then I felt him erupting inside me. I felt the power of his orgasm. With a relieved sigh, I closed my eyes and threw an arm over them. Gradually, he pulled out. He kissed my neck, in between my boobs, my pelvic bone.

"Nice kitty," he murmured as he wiped away the evidence of our afternoon romp. Then he lifted me into his arms and deposited me on the bed. "We should have done it here from the start. If we had, you wouldn't be suffering from rug burn right now." He chuckled.

More than anything, I just wanted to sleep for a bit, preferably in his arms. How he had the energy to lift me or stand, I couldn't imagine. Then, he stumbled a little. "Whew, too much blood south of the border for this," he joked as he climbed onto the bed next to me. As he wrapped his arms around me, he asked, "Can we just nap here…like this…for a little while?"

Still worn out, I couldn't speak. I just nodded my head. He knew, since his head was on top of mine. One hand held mine under the pillow. The other cupped my breast and tucked under me. His arm was positioned so that he could haul me closer the minute he felt too much space between us. *So nice.* That was my last thought before sleep claimed me.

Chapter 5

When I woke, the morning of our second full day at sea, I was surprised to discover that I was alone. It took me a moment to process it. I grabbed a bathrobe from the closet, and found that the bathroom was empty. I could see from where I was standing that he wasn't on the balcony. Before I could ponder what to do next, I heard that all too familiar card in the door.

Turning to smile in greeting, I caught Mr. BE just as he was stumbling through the door. "I'm never going to get my sea legs," he joked.

In his hand he had one plate that was heaping full of some of our favorite breakfast foods. Then he turned around and picked up another plate and a heaping bowl of fruit salad. My smile was genuine and effortless.

"I was hoping we could have breakfast in bed and lay low for little bit. I guess the waves are bothering me more than I thought," he said. "Plus, it's just a day of nothing before we hit Grand Turk in the morning."

Nodding, I brought the food to the bed. "Wow," I said, "you must have taken just a few of everything. It's all my favorites."

He smiled. "I know. I paid attention." Then he lowered himself to the edge of the bed. He seemed worn out and I had to admit, it was probably my fault for not letting him rest more at night. I was being too selfish and all the while he's been struggling with motion sickness and totally worn out.

"Relax," I suggested. "It's a perfect day to lounge around. If I want sun, I'll go out on the balcony. If you want me to lay with you, I will. Let's eat before it gets cold."

I meant everything I said, but suddenly I had no idea where it came from. It was, sensitive, caring, bordering on nurturing and maternal. Gawd, if it had been that lawyer asking me to sleep in when I wanted to be up enjoying the party on the lido deck, I probably would have told him to fuck off and catch up when he could. I hadn't even hung around for Jolie. Thank goodness, because if I had, I might have missed meeting this man.

Shake it off! Four days. That's all that's left. Just live in the moment with Mr. BE. I hated that I had to keep reminding myself. Yet, I loved this…my best regroup ever, even if I wasn't regrouping with Jolie. Hell, it didn't matter. We weren't on a time schedule. We could just stay a few extra days in Charleston if we wanted. We had nothing to rush back to.

So we sat and ate. I fed him some. He did the same for me. When the food had disappeared, he nestled down in the pillows.

"Sleepy," he said, quietly. He started to close his eyes. "I just need a little nap. Then we can do whatever you want. You don't even have to wait here. I can meet you somewhere…" His voice trailed off.

"Now what kind of wife would I be if I just left you when you weren't feeling well? Nah. I'll stick around. I may even nap with you," I said.

A smiled spread across his lips. He reached out and grazed my face with the back of his hand. "You are the perfect wife," he said. "I'll never have better." Then he closed his eyes and fell asleep.

While he slept, I loaded pictures onto the laptop. I uploaded several that I sent to different magazines. Then I took some shots of him sleeping. There was something so alluring about him, with the light scruff he had growing on his face, the thick dark lashes that were too pretty to belong to any man, and the way his biceps bulged under the t-shirt. There was plenty of time for me to take a luxurious shower, to apply the minimal amount of makeup, the gross quantities of sunblock, and pull my hair up into a messy bun.

As lunchtime arrived, it was my turn to go and bring back some food for us. Surely he would awaken hungry in a short period of time. When he did, I wanted to make sure he was as well cared for as he had done for me. While I knew that I could have ordered room service, I also knew how disruptive and noisy it was for me to call, then for them to arrive and bang on the door. There would be the balancing act while signing for the food, and let's not forget the tip. Plus, the selection was greater in Windows on the Sea buffet than it was on the limited room service menu.

Just as I walked in the door with our plates and set them on the coffee table, he began to awaken. "That was quite the nap," I commented. "Hope you are hungry."

He smiled and nodded. "I'm starving. We'll need to get ice cream after this." Then he reached for the grilled ham and cheese I picked up for him at the deli.

Soon we were having fun, joking, playing, and it of course turned into one of my passions. The camera was out and I was recording every moment of this. What I loved was the spontaneity of it all. Instead of focusing and pausing, it was all point and shoot. Periodically, I would check and see if I was getting anything worth saving. Oh, I was. I captured this look on his face, this playful adoration as we were rolling around on the bed. It was perfect. He might be gifting me paintings and jewelry, but this was what I could give him for forever. He would have these photographs on the SD card to always remember.

Emma Nichols

We finally started dressing for dinner. "What are you wearing tonight?" He asked casually.

Without saying a word, I pulled the only other cocktail dress I had packed. The hem ended just a few inches over the knee. Around the bottom of the all black dress was a glittery silver butterfly pattern. It had a dangerously low back. And I loved how it looked with the black-strapped heels that connected above the ankle.

"Hmmm," he said as he turned the dress around on the hanger. "I like it, but I don't love it."

"Thanks," I responded icily. I thrive on compliments and get a little tense when I receive unwarranted criticisms. I turned away to start dressing despite his lackluster enthusiasm. The night was off to a bad start. My back was to him and it would stay that way until I managed to get my seething anger under control. One by one, I showed him each and every one of the dresses we had picked together. Each time, he made a face that suggested he was unimpressed. My ego was taking a blow. Suddenly my confidence was in the toilet. I had run out of options. With my head down, I faced away from him once more.

Wrapping one arm around me, I stiffened. Then the second arm came around and it was holding a beautiful blue cocktail dress. "I just thought this one would go better with our eyes, and your ring, and my dress shirt," he said with a shrug. "Of course, if you hate it, I'll return it." He started to pull back and take the dress from my view.

Naturally, I snatched it from his hand. "I love it," I said slowly. I had always worn my dark hair long. Sometimes I let the natural waves take over, other times I straightened the heck out of it. Lately, I had been letting my eyes do the talking. As eyes went, I had always liked mine. They were blue…deep blue. They turned up on the outside so that I always looked happy. At the moment, they were filled with tears. "You bought me a dress." I held it in my hands and touched the fabric. It was flowing and sheer and long. It made me think of something that Helen of Troy would wear. It may have been love at first sight. "You bought me a dress?" I just kept petting it and staring at it.

"Yes, I bought you a dress. I'll take you to dinner if you put it on," he urged.

Holding the dress against me I whipped around and looked at him. With a suggestive eyebrow raised, I asked, "What if I take everything off?"

Laughing, he responded, "I'll show you that tonight. First, we eat." He patted my butt to get me moving. "I'm just going to wait out on the balcony. I seem to be a bit…distracting."

Already I was biting my lip. It was going to be long night. Fine. Two could play this game. Again I found myself wearing pasties and a teeny tiny thong. Tonight it would be black with a star charm holding it all together in the back. That should do it. Putting the finishing touches on my hair and makeup, we finally left the room.

Glancing at his watch, he said, "We still have a good hour before we should hit the line for dinner. What would you like to do?"

Laughing, I hooked my arm through his. "Let's go, handsome. We have to live a lifetime in one week. We're going to do it all."

We exited onto the promenade deck and I lead him all the way to the sushi bar. Every night from 5-8pm there was a selection of sushi. It was only two different kinds of rolls, but it was all we could eat. Over the course of the week, I planned to make them regret that. Starting now.

"I don't eat sushi," he said while demonstrating his best full body shudder.

"You do now," I said. I released his arm to step toward the sushi bar. Suddenly, he caught on. They would only give each person four pieces of sushi. As a hors d'oeuvre, it was only a taste for me. I needed his, too.

Playing along, he asked, "So, do I like ginger?"

Smirking, I said, "No, you hate ginger."

"How do I feel about wasabi?" He asked with a straight face and raised eyebrows.

Chuckling, I said, "You *love* wasabi!" Then I placed a healthy scoop on both plates.

We found an open window seat and I immediately sat down and patted the spot beside me. Smiling, he joined me. It was off to the side, out of the line of sight, hidden almost completely by the photography background set up. With that kind of set up, it was easy enough to rub against his leg, to run my hand along his inner thigh, to lean in and speak in a low seductive voice in his ear under the guise of too much background noise.

It was working. I could see him getting excited. It was evident in the way he shifted in his seat. It was obvious in the way that he covered his groin with the plate. Still, I needed to up the ante. Standing, I bent low over him to collect his plate. At the angle I was bending, I had no doubt that he could see straight down my dress. I gazed at his face just to be sure. Yup. He was transfixed, completely frozen as he stared at my goodies.

"Baby, can I take that plate for you?" I asked innocently. "They won't let us bring it in the casino."

At first, he started to pass me the plate without thinking, and then he shook his head as if to break the trance and gripped it even tighter.

Emma Nichols

"I'm just going to hold onto it for a minute," he said breathlessly.

Blinking, I looked at him and asked, "Have you reconsidered your stance on sushi?"

Shaking his head he closed his eyes for a moment. He leaned over and held his head in his hands. From where I stood, I could hear that he was mumbling something. I sat down quickly, concerned.

"What?" I asked. "What are you saying?" Reaching out, I grabbed his forearm with my hand.

"Just mumbling things that are major turnoffs," he said with a sly look. "It helps…so I don't have to sit around with a plate in my lap all night." He smirked.

Standing, I smiled. "Well, you take all the time you need. I'm going to the casino. Will you join me?"

"Soon, babe," he assured me.

The torture continued into dinner. The power had definitely shifted. It felt…great. I was working hard to keep it that way, too. This time, instead of playing footsies under the table, rather than run a hand up and down his thigh, I had intentionally moved my chair just out of his reach. He noticed immediately and raised an eyebrow.

Smiling at him, I made small talk with the woman seated next to me. Her husband was engrossed in something on his phone. I didn't envy him the shock when he received that phone bill. Cellular at sea is not cheap. I once forgot to turn off the data on my cellphone on a cruise, and even though I didn't make any calls or send any text messages, after five days at sea, I had accrued a $1300 bill. So I made nice with the lonely wife. When I glanced over at Mr. BE, he was making nice with a lonely wife, too.

She was talking to him, then laughing and touching his arm. That was all I needed to see. It was as effective as a punch to the gut. I stood quickly, and mumbled some excuse about why I had to leave immediately. Really, I don't know what I said. I don't remember. I wasn't paying attention when the words escaped my lips. I wasn't thinking anything other than *I have to get out of here. Right. Now.*

There may have been some stumbling involved as I tried to get my chair pushed back and my heel caught on the carpeting. There may have been some tears in my eyes that blurred my vision. I was wearing his dress, his earrings…his ring. I just wanted it off. All of it needed to be off…immediately.

When I reached the elevator, I stomped my foot, completely disgusted with my reaction. What would I do now? I didn't have a key to his stateroom. I had borrowed his that he left on the vanity when I picked up lunch. I had moved out of the cabin I shared with Jolie. If I went

Emma Nichols

back, I could be interrupting something. Or, worse, I would have to tell her what happened. Two lone tears trickled down my face. Sniffling, I wiped them away as quickly as possible. What had happened? He spoke to another woman, she touched him, and he didn't do anything about it. Were all men that stupid?

Circling, I watched the elevator lights. "Fuck. How hard is it to get an elevator around here?" Head bent, I began rubbing my temples. So lost in thought, I never heard him coming up behind me. My leg up in our power struggle was completely gone. Just as I circled around once more, I walked right into him. Instead of being relieved, I cried harder.

"Whoa. What's going on?" He asked concerned.

"Nothing. I'm not feeling well. I just needed some air and space and…and time," I said as I spoke into his chest. Somehow, I just couldn't meet his eyes. I couldn't reveal the hurt and pain I felt. Worse, I felt such shame. Was I really that pathetic, that the first guy who came along and seemed decent evoked immediate feelings from me? It made no sense.

"Come eat dinner," he urged. "You'll feel better. I'll be the most devoted husband ever."

Shaking my head, I pulled away from him and hugged myself. "Can I get the room key? I just want to go…get changed…"

"What if I don't give it to you?" He asked, testing me.

"Then I give you back your ring, the earrings, and send the dress back later. I'll go stay in my own cabin with Jolie." I raised an eyebrow at him, a visual suggestion that he pause and decide what he was going to do.

Sighing, he started to pass me the card. "Let's go back to the room. We'll order room service. I'm starving." He frowned as he laid his hand on my lower back and directed me toward the open elevator. Only this time, the hand on my lower back felt unwelcome and it was all I could do to not shake him off, shove him away.

A horrible thought occurred to me. This wasn't about my pride. If it was, I simply would have made every man within 20 feet fall for me, start giving me the eyes. I could do that. I was young, attractive, and wearing a virtually transparent dress. If it were about pride, I'd be making him sorry, making him want me, making him regret that he ever let another woman lay a hand on him…even if it was only his forearm. Alas, this seemed to be about something much more involved, like my heart.

My head was down as we walked onto the elevator. Still, I noticed that he had hit the button for the lido deck instead of the Atlantic. Embarrassed as I was, I didn't trust myself to speak, to protest, or to object. For now, I would simply go along with whatever he had in mind. So I waited dutifully for him to lay a hand on my back and direct me where he wanted to go. I plodded along as he brought us to the buffet. I watched with fascination as he made me a hot tea.

"This should soothe you some," he said quietly, "since my hugs aren't doing the trick tonight." He passed me the mug and watched my face for a reaction.

"Thank you," I mumbled quietly. This was such a humbling experience. Really, I didn't like it one bit. Worse, I couldn't find a logical reason for my reaction.

"Let's get food to go," he said, "unless you want to stay here to eat."

Looking up at him, I wondered what I saw. Was this his version of contrite? Was he hurting, too? There was a pain in his eyes that I didn't recognize. "I'm…sorry," I managed to grit out. "I'm sure I overreacted. Let's sit here, have a nice quiet dinner, and salvage our night."

Staring at me for a moment, the pain gradually disappeared and was replaced by hope. He pulled me close, careful to not spill my tea, and kissed my head enthusiastically a few times. "I'm sorry, too," he said. "I didn't mean to hurt you, but I'd be lying if I didn't admit to trying to make you a bit jealous." Glancing around, he seemed to notice that we were drawing more attention than he was comfortable with. He reached out, turned me toward an empty table for two near the windows and once again placed a hand on my lower back.

This time, I felt the warmth and comfort that I usually did. It did more to elevate my spirits than the tea. We sat and he spoke immediately. I watched and waited while sipping the Earl Grey.

"You are so…amazing and beautiful. You drive me absolutely wild. Now, I know we said that this was to be living in the week, in the moment; I guess I managed to get caught up in all of it. Suddenly, it was as though you really were my wife, as though you really were mine. That changed everything. Let's not forget again. More than that…let's just treat each other right. No more games. No more competitions"

My eyebrows rose and I blushed some. He was definitely onto me. He might just be my soul mate. Alas, I'd never know. "Sounds good," I said honestly. For some reason, with him, I had lost my edge. No sense in competing if I wasn't going to win.

The mug was nearly empty, but my heart was full. We were not only going to salvage the night, but the rest of the week. We weren't back on track as much as we had found our groove.

With that, we headed to the buffet lines. "I'll meet you back here," I said happily. "I have to teach this buffet a lesson." I winked at him and walked away. Without looking back, I already knew he was staring at my butt through the dress. This time it wasn't a game. I really did want him to want more.

As we finished up dinner, he looked at me from across the table. "So, do you want to see a show?" He asked. "We could go to the comedy club."

I shook my head as I stared at him over the salted rim of my margarita. He would hit on the perfect end to our day eventually.

"We could go to the casino and gamble this time? I think I'm finally accustomed to you in that dress. What was I thinking?" He smiled playfully.

"You have excellent taste in dresses. And women. By the way, in case you haven't figured it out yet, you've peaked." I beamed.

"Peaked?" He looked confused.

"Sadly, you are completely doomed. You will never find another woman like me. You might just as well resign yourself to a life of celibacy now. Forever will I be the measure for all the others." I bit my lip to keep from laughing.

"Well, then I guess it's a good thing I married you. Now wife, what would you like to do tonight? I will never understand the complexities of your crafty little mind," he said, and then bowed in deference.

"Let me show you how I think we should end our night," I said as I stood. I reached out, offering him my hand, the good one, the one with the ring on it.

His hand, grasped mine for a moment, ran his thumb over my fingers, pausing just under the ring. He smiled. "I chose well," he said quietly, suddenly more serious than the moment merited.

"The ring is absolutely beautiful," I admitted, squeezing his hand a little tighter.

Standing, he looked me in the eyes, cupped the side of my face with his free hand and said, "I meant you." Then he kissed me, gently, sincerely, openly…like a man kisses the woman he loves.

It took my breath away. It made my heart beat wildly. Mostly, I walked around numbly for a bit. When I finally was thinking straight again, we were in the hot tub and he was running a hand up and down my inner thigh.

"Something I said," he asked innocently before winking at me. "Or, I'd like to believe it was something I did."

That was pretty much all the inciting I needed. I was going to make him forget, too. He would forget every woman who came before me, every moment that I wasn't a part of, every dream he had that didn't include me. Starting now.

Emma Nichols

Propelling him across the hot tub, I finally noticed that we had the entire Serenity spa to ourselves. Even the towel boy was long gone. There was no one on the deck above us, no movement at all. It was as though we had the entire ship to ourselves and I was determined to make the most of it.

Running my hand up his inner thing like he had done to mine, I watched as he went from relaxed to anticipatory. It only took a second for me to reach under his swim trunks and free him from the mesh lining. He had a semi, but I knew that I could fix that. By now, I had him so well trained that it barely took more than a couple of strokes of my hand for him to be eager and at the ready.

Wrapping my legs around his waist, I leaned back and floated against him. He ran a hand over my pelvic bone and down over my eager wet opening. I think he wanted me to object, to claim some false modesty, but that wasn't me. Instead, I gave him a brazen look, dared him to do it.

Without even glancing about first, he slipped my bikini bottom aside, lowered the front of his trunks, and quickly slid inside me. I sat up, on his lap and went to work. Never have I been more proud of his daring. The sheer excitement over possibly getting caught thrilled both of us. It didn't take long for either of us to achieve our orgasm. We quickly adjusted our suits so that no one would ever suspect the passion that had just passed between us.

"I've never been this horny before…not even when I was teenager. I swear…I am ready for you the moment you look at me with those lustful eyes he, "murmured into my ear as he nuzzled me close on his lap. "I don't understand it."

Though I might have made suggestions earlier or discussed my suspicions, this time I knew to stay focused. We had mere days left together. "Let's not question it. Let's just be."

"I can live with that," he said against my neck. Then he chuckled at a joke I didn't understand.

Chapter 6

When I opened my eyes, Mr. BE was staring down at me smiling. He was propped on an elbow and began stroking my cheek with the back of his other hand. "Morning, gorgeous," he said quietly. "We're in Grand Turk."

Bounding from the bed, I threw on the bathrobe. "Oh my God! What time is it?" I ran to the balcony and threw open the door. Sure enough, we were docked. Judging by the colors, it was definitely the Caribbean. All the buildings were in shades of pink, blue, green, and peach. There was a big beach with white lounge chairs in neat rows across it. "Ah," I said with a sigh.

Walking back into the room, I dropped the bathrobe and my panties while I walked over to my bag. After rummaging around in it for a moment, I found what I was looking for, my black bikini. He cleared his throat.

"It'd be a shame for that beautiful naked body to go to waste," he murmured as he walked over to me and dropped his boxers.

"Yeah?" I said with a smile.

"Look," he said, showing me the watch on his wrist. "It's only 7am.

We can't even debark until 9am. We don't have to be back on board until 4:30pm…" He began caressing my naked skin. Soon, I was covered in goose bumps and shaking with need.

His head bent as he began kissing me. He was playful at first, then with a growing sense of urgency. He bent his head further as he began to lap at my nipples, then suck, and finally applied just the right amount of pressure with his teeth. We were just about to climb onto the bed when there was a knock at the door.

"Really?" He asked aloud. "Bathrobe," he said to me, pointing to the one on the floor near the balcony door.

"What about you?" I asked.

"I'll grab one from the closet," he said with a shrug. Then he turned toward me. "Not that I'll be able to close it," he said with a chuckle.

Pulling open the closet, he took the one remaining robe and slid into it before tightening the belt around his waist. With his erection poking out of it, I couldn't help but chuckle as I righted my robe and watched him answer the door.

"Hey," Jolie began when he had the door propped open two or three inches. "so which excursion did you sign up for?"

"Jolie, we haven't even managed to get up yet," he said with an edge of frustration to his voice.

After glancing down briefly, she looked him in the eyes once more. "You seem to have gotten up just fine." She crossed her arms over her chest.

With a giant sigh, he stepped aside and let her in. "I'm going to go take a shower," he said to me. "A really cold shower." Then he went into the bathroom and shut the door behind him.

"Nice, Jolie. Thanks for that," I said with a smirk.

She shrugged. "I'm just killing time. I haven't seen you much and I thought we were planning our next move," she said sadly.

"Who hurt you?" I asked. Jolie never missed me as much as she did when someone let her down.

"Her name was Misty. She was perfect…hot body, great smile, and an awesome sex drive. Then I saw her with someone else at breakfast." She sat heavily on the bed.

"You'll be fine. This is just fun, remember?" I smiled at her.

With a scowl, she said, "I remember. Do you? Because you two seem pretty hot and heavy. You two are breaking all the rules."

Smirking I said, "Rules are meant to be broken. Cheer up. And unless you have any objections…let's move to Vegas. I think we're just the right age for it. Plus, it's not the kind of place we'd ever want to settle down. What do you think?"

Jolie seemed to be trying out the idea in her mind. Slowly she smiled. "Yeah, I can see that." She laughed for a moment. "Sin the Vixen in Vegas. I can't wait." Standing, she looked at me and went in for a hug. "Okay, maybe I'll see you two in Grand Turk."

Then she headed to the door. "Bye, handsome mystery man!" She shouted at the bathroom door as she headed out of the stateroom.

I chuckled. There wasn't much else to do in that situation. "Are you clean?" I asked, as I opened the door and leaned into the bathroom.

Standing there with a towel wrapped around his waist, he smirked at me. "As a matter of fact, yes I am," he responded.

"Good," I said, "because I'm really dirty." Then I knelt down in front of him and pulled the towel off of his hips. Taking him in both hands, I opened my mouth wide. This was going to be a great day.

We had a nice quiet breakfast. He was super calm, more relaxed than I had ever seen him. Naturally, I felt the need to comment on it. "Having the testosterone sucked out of you is a good look for you," I joked.

He heaved a completely euphoric sigh. "You are a good look for me,"

Emma Nichols

Mr. BE said seriously. He took my hands in his. "Thank you for this week," he said staring intently in my eyes. "You will never understand how much this means to me." He broke the stare and looked away.

I studied him. What was going on? Was he hurting like I had been? "Listen, you've done wonders for me, too," I said. It was too serious. I needed to have fun. "Let's go do Grand Turk." I nodded to the shore from the lido deck.

"Where do you want to go?" He asked with a questioning face.

Smiling, I responded, "Wherever our feet take us."

Those feet…they really knew where to go. Since it was early and a nice comfortable temperature when we debarked, we decided to do some sightseeing first. Unlike past stops in the Bahamas on previous cruises, Grand Turk was beautiful. Everything was new and well maintained. There was tons of shopping, and I don't mean souvenirs, I mean real shopping…like major name brand companies and designers. It was so nice that we couldn't even find a souvenir lighter for the fancy cigar he had hoped to light. The duty free shop was incredible…an amazing selection of perfumes, makeup, liquor, and jewelry. I wandered around sniffing and touching until Mr. BE caught up to me.

"Try this one," he said as he squirted me with a tester.

I was taken aback. "That was worse than walking through a Macy's," I complained. Then I sniffed my arm and all was forgiven. "What is that? I love it."

"Bulgari," he announced proudly. Then he walked away. I watched him put the tester back, then grab the biggest bottle they had off the shelf.

Shaking my head, I turned my attention to a guidebook. Traveling the Caribbean was one of my many dreams. Maybe I should pick the book up for future getaways with Jolie. Before I could make that decision, he was ready to try another store.

We went to a series of stores where he would wander off, leaving me to shop on my own and then catch up with me later. I tried not to be too nosy…no man wants that kind of wife, but I'd be lying if I didn't admit that I was a bit curious. Okay…more than a bit. When he'd catch me looking…bordering on peeking…he'd laugh and tell me that it was a surprise.

Apparently I need to be the kind of wife that is into surprises instead of a spoilsport. To get my mind off the packages, I suggested that we stop at the first bar we found to get a drink…and maybe a snack. "You're starting to wear out. I can feel it. Your enthusiasm for the day is waning. Let's stop shopping and enjoy some sun and beach. I saw some beach chairs from the boat. Let's find them!" I said eagerly.

"Whew. I mean, it's getting hot and I would love a drink. And to see you in that bikini…" He laughed.

Hooking my arm through his we turned a corner…and there it was: Margaritaville! "You have got to be kidding me!" Then I squealed like the girl I am and started tugging him behind me. "We have to go here!"

"What's so special about Margaritaville?" He asked. "I was rather hoping we'd find some quiet little beach bar…" He shrugged.

"You will love this. I promise," I assured him as I dragged him to the door. We paused for a moment as I snapped a few pictures of him in front of the parrot, next to the sign, and in front of the fountain. Then, we entered through the store.

The Grand Turk Margaritaville was so different than what I expected. Of course, I had only been to one previously in Myrtle Beach. This one had a pool. People were lounging around, sipping drinks, working on their tans in this gorgeous tropical location. More than anything, I was excited to join them.

"How's your skin?" I asked.

"Soft as a baby's bottom. What kind of question is that?" He asked with a laugh.

Shaking my head, I said, "I mean do you burn easily. I don't want you getting skin cancer." I pulled out the bottle of SPF 30 I had in my bag and started applying it liberally while we stood off to the side. "Where do you want to sit?"

Mr. BE glanced around. "I'm torn," he said finally. "I mean over there is the beach and all those really inviting lounge chairs. Over here, the pool, the radio station, the party atmosphere. What if we sit over here on the edge of the pool so we can enjoy both?"

"Perfect," I said sincerely.

We dropped our bags, I sat down and he went to the bar to get us drinks. While he was gone, I laid out our towels, took off my sundress, and sat on the chair. I pulled the lotion out and began to slather it on my shoulders and my chest. Then I felt strong hands on my back and smiled as I relaxed into it. "Thank you, handsome, " I said as I grabbed his wrist to kiss his fingertips. That's when I realized that I didn't know those fingers. To begin with, this guy was a nail biter. Mr. BE had beautiful hands.

Suddenly I was holding the wrist very differently, like it disgusted me. I stood very slowly, so as not to cause a scene, and then I turned to look at the guy who just imagined he could run his hands over my body without permission. There was no holding back. I could feel the look of disgust on my face. "What the hell do you think you are doing?" I asked through gritted teeth. "You don't just lay your hands on a woman you don't know. That is assault. Had your hands gone lower, I could probably make a case for sexual assault." Crossing my arms over my chest, I suddenly felt very exposed.

He opened his mouth to speak, but before he could, I interrupted. "I don't need to hear anything…not even an apology. Just go away before my husband gets back with our drinks."

It was too late. Mr. BE was back. He passed me a huge margarita in a blender cup. Normally, I would have been all excited over the souvenir cup, but the tension was such that I could have cut it with a knife. I started to pack up our beach towels and the sunblock into the beach bag, but he gestured for me to stop. So I did.

The guys were having a standoff, staring each other down, seeing who was going to break first. They seemed to be equally matched size wise, but after watching the Rocky films, I knew better than to place my money on the big guy. Finally, the tension was broken when the handsy dude offered to buy Mr. BE a drink.

"Sure," he said, unimpressed. Then he gestured to me and said, "Come on, babe." He took the beach bag from me. It seemed to be something that he would have done anyway, not a show of ownership. I have to tell you, I appreciated it. The weight of the bag, those straps cutting into my shoulder, it was a worry of the past. I had a man now, a husband even, to help with the heavy lifting. A woman could get used to this.

Know what else I could get used to? The Caribbean. The bar looked like something out of a movie or print ad even. It was this open-air bar with a grass roof. The sky was gorgeous. The temperature was divine. I just loved everything about the place, the moment, and maybe even a little…the man I was with.

So we stood at the bar and the man ordered a shot of tequila. Mr. BE did the same. The gauntlet had been thrown. Pride was at stake. I started sucking down my margarita. This could be a long day.

They went shot for shot while I drank this never ending super strong margarita. After a while, I realized why it seemed to be never ending. The bartender kept filling it. When I looked at him questioningly, he responded, "You're going to need it." Then he nodded at the men trying to best each other in a drinking challenge.

Sighing, I said, "You're right. Thank you."

By the time we made it back to the boat for dinner, I was stumbling and my stomach was churning. We went directly to the buffet where my husband, in his great wisdom, loaded a plate with food for him and rolls for me. He made me a hot tea, and filled his own glass with this half lemonade, half sweet tea mixture that he claimed was very tasty.

After making our way back to the room, I collapsed on the bed. Though I was sure there was nothing sexy about my posture or pose, my care at the moment was limited to non-existent. Already I was faced with the challenge of getting some much needed sleep when every time I closed my eyes, the room spun out of control.

"I don't get it," I mourned. "I'm a responsible drinker. How did this happen?" Then, when I felt my stomach contents threatening to make a return trip, I rushed to the bathroom.

Sitting on the cool floor felt nice, of course it if hadn't been a bumpy faux tiled floor, it would have been even nicer. In the bedroom, I could hear Mr. BE eating his meal. It didn't make any sense. He had been drinking longer and harder than I had to win. Yet he seemed completely sober. A minute later, he peeked in to check on me.

"Babe, you okay? You need me to hold your hair or rub your back?" His voice was filled with concern.

Somehow, I managed to shake my head. That proved to be a big mistake that had me scrambling to my knees to launch my stomach contents into the toilet. I'm sure it was really attractive. Only, when I was finally aware of something other than the lurching and cramping of my stomach, I realized that despite my original protest, he was rubbing my back and holding back my hair.

After wiping my mouth with a towel and blowing my nose, I looked at him sadly and joked, "Well, you have the vows down."

"The vows?" He asked with a confused look.

"Yeah, you know…in sickness and in health." I gave him a weak smile.

Leaning in, he kissed me on the forehead. "Let's give you a shower and put you to bed," he suggested.

After considering his words, I nodded and let him help me out of my clothes. All these other times between us had been so sexy. Every day had been filled with passion and heat. For once, it was nice to experience some tender loving care.

He turned the water on and tested it, showing me yet another facet of his personality. This had been such a revealing day. The more I knew about him, the more I liked him. What wasn't there to like?

Moments later, he surprised me by undressing and joining me. I started to open my mouth, but he silenced me with a finger to my lips. "This isn't a time for sex, babe. I just wanted to be in here to help wash you, to steady you, to keep you safe. There will be plenty of time for you show your appreciation later. For now, let me show you how much I care," he said gently.

Emma Nichols

It's a good thing we were in the shower, otherwise he would have known that some of the water running down my cheeks didn't come from the plumbing.

Chapter 7

The drinking seemed like a good idea at the time. Only, now, as I woke back in our stateroom with my head pounding and no idea what time of day it was, I began to reconsider my reasoning. I glanced around with one eye open while holding my pounding head. There he was, the picture of sobriety, sitting on the couch to my left reading a book.

Slowly, I sat up. "How?" I asked.

He chuckled. "How did you get here?" He set the book down and stood to join me in bed. He crawled across the cool white sheets until he was beside me, smiling. "You walked…mostly. I tucked you in after the shower."

"Mmm…what time is it?" I asked frightened.

"Don't worry. You didn't miss much. You woke in time to have breakfast before they close the buffet," he said as he stroked my back.

Making a face, I said, "I don't know about that."

"Trust me," he said. "You don't want to skip a meal right now. We'll get you loads of Coke to settle that stomach and some rolls. You'll be a new woman." He nuzzled my neck after brushing some hair away.

Sighing blissfully despite my rolling stomach, I said, "Okay. Talk me into it…but explain one thing first?"

Kissing my ring hand, he said, "Anything."

"How is it you aren't sick? You drank way more than I did." I crossed my arms over my chest.

Mr. BE chuckled. "Did I?" He asked. I looked at him suspiciously. Chuckling harder, he said, "What? You've never seen *Coyote Ugly?* I spit it out while drinking my chaser. Don't worry, Big Dumb and Ugly never figured it out either. He won't be bothering you anymore." He winked at me.

"Smart and handsome," I marveled. "Can I pick a husband or what?" Before he could answer, ruin the moment with some remark, I threw my arms around his neck and pressed my body against him. After a few moments, I finally pulled myself away. There was something so perfect about being in his arms. When he held me at night as I drifted off to sleep, when he hugged me close when I was awake, having his hand on my lower back as we walked along…somehow his touch made me feel complete, like a part of me that I had never realized was missing had at last returned. With a sigh, I threw back the covers and stood as soon as my feet hit the floor. I stretched and said, "So, what shall we do today."

Smiling wide, he said, "After yesterday, I thought we could use some quiet alone time. Don't worry; I made sure to make it special."

Looking at him sideways, I asked, "What have you done?"

Shaking his head, he responded, "It's a surprise. Go get ready."

He was right…about everything. For the first time in my life, I lost nothing by someone else being right. Instead, I had everything to gain. The shore excursion in Half Moon Cay was absolutely perfect.

By the time I was out of the shower, Mr. BE had the beach bag packed. "I know that technically the bag is yours, but as your wife, don't I get some kind of peeking privileges?"

"Not when your peeking interferes with my surprising. I've been planning this for two days, don't ruin it," he said. "I promise, it will be completely worth your while. Better still, you don't have long to wait."

We had a light breakfast, which was just what I needed…some toast on the belly, a lot of tea, and a couple of Ibuprofen. It was well rounded. Then we went to line up for the boat to the private island. In a perfect world, I would own a private Caribbean island…with a dock…for my yacht. In this world, my yacht is a cruise ship and I'm borrowing their island. Still, it's not a bad way to live.

As we rode the boat over, he shifted the bag a few times. "Want me to carry it?" I asked. "I know how it can cut into a shoulder."

"Nah, I've got it," he said, but he sounded a bit tired.

"Did you get any sleep, or did I keep you up for all the wrong reasons last night?" I asked as I worried over him.

That seemed to be enough for him to shake off whatever was bothering him. "Nah, I'm good," he said. Then he reached over and held my hand. "We are going to have such a special day."

Nodding, I agreed, "We sure are." Then I felt a little guilty. "Listen, I know our time is limited. I'm so sorry for ruining even a moment of it yesterday." I looked down, unable to meet his eyes.

A gentle finger lifted my chin and he said softly, "For better or worse, remember?" Then with a chuckle he said, "Or in our case…you promised me the boring stuff, too."

Naturally, I threw myself into his arms at that point. I had to. Who else would want the boring stuff? I was going to have to make today super special.

When we landed, we checked in and were taken to our bungalow for the day. It had a table and chairs set up, some lounge chairs, an air conditioner and food. There were chips and salsa, which I think is a perfectly yummy snack. There were plenty of other comforts. I looked around and smiled at him in approval.

"Listen," he began, "I considered going fancier, but it seemed that all the more expensive options came with help and I wanted you all to myself." He crushed me against his chest.

I was jumping up and down like a kid as I asked the next question. Past experience had taught me that cute…definitely opened doors. In this case, I was hoping it would open bags…the ones he was carrying in particular. "Is it surprise time yet?" I asked. For effect, I batted my eyelashes at him.

Sighing happily, he said, "I suppose so." Opening the beach bag, he fumbled around. "Here are some extra goodies I had them pack for us." Then he began pulling out a few containers of food…some grapes, and strawberries. He had a container of whipped cream that made me smirk. Next he pulled out some of my favorites. I had grown really attached to their version of potato salad and seemed to eat it at least once a day. There were sandwiches and pickles. There was even a special chocolate mousse dessert.

"You thought of everything!" I exclaimed happily.

Emma Nichols

"I did more than that," he said beaming. "Time for presents." He pulled out a box that I recognized from the duty free shop in Grand Turk. "I love this perfume on you. Wear it now and then and think of me, okay?" He passed me the J'adore he had sprayed on me the day before. The scent had lingered on me all day. It was absolutely perfect.

"Thank you," I said, "I love it." Then I opened the box and pulled it out, ready to spray some on.

"Wait!" He said, using his hand to halt my action. "These go with it." He pulled out a small gift bag.

My curiosity was piqued. I peered inside and laughed. Apparently, he had rather liked my selection of panties. Now he was adding to the collection. It was a scarlet thong, like the rest I owned…a patch of nylon…a couple of thin scarlet strings, and it was all connected with a silver heart.

"You need to wear them together," he said seductively. "I now proclaim today P&P Day."

"P&P?" I questioned.

"Yes," he said, leaning in for a kiss, "Panties and Perfume. You game?" Then he grazed my lips with his and I already wanted more.

"Give me a minute to think about it," I joked as I began to pull off my sundress and slip off the panties I had put on that morning.

He leaned against the table, appreciating the view. Tugging on his chin, his look was intense. "I hope you know it's all I can do to just look right now," he said.

Standing there in nothing but the panties he gave me, I slowly raised my arms and released my ponytail, shaking it out and letting it cascade down my back and over my shoulders. I turned around and gave him a view from the back, bending completely over to fluff my hair. Then, while bent over, I glanced back at him and asked, "What's stopping you?"

It was a challenge and he took it as such. Though I wasn't looking, I heard the sound of his belt being undone, his shorts hitting the floor, and the elastic snapping under his fingers. Already, I could feel my body growing ready for him. I was on fire, pulsing. The sound of his steps closing the distance between had me all but panting for him. He didn't stop walking until he was against me, pressing his hot throbbing cock against my wet opening. His thumb reached in and flicked the thong aside while caressing each butt cheek with one hand. When he finally came around to the inner thigh area, he spread my legs slightly and said quietly, "What would you like?"

Suddenly I was aware that I had been holding my breath. Exhaling slowly, I nearly whimpered. "In me. In me, please. Right now."

There was a brief pause before he responded, "Okay, but only because you said 'please.'" Then he chuckled as he leaned over and whispered in my ear, "Breathe, baby."

Just as I inhaled, filling my lungs with air, he filled my vag with his hot erection. I couldn't get enough. Soon I was bucking against him. He grabbed my hips and held on, pushing again and again. We found our rhythm. It didn't take long before I was panting and crying out and with the intensity of the last thrust, I knew he had climaxed, too.

We collapsed on the floor right there on a pile of beach blankets. "Hold me?" I asked. In answer, he pulled me closer, fit my body to his, and spooned me like it was his job. No wonder I fell asleep.

The rest of the day was more of the same, except for when we left the bungalow to swim. The water was crystal clear. The temperature was perfect. There was a quiet understanding between us, or maybe he was just quiet. He seemed lost in thought. I understood. I was, too.

We played some in the water, splashing around, trying to chase each other. It didn't last long. "Water and sun are making me tired," he complained. "Let's settle in on some of the blankets and eat. What do you think?"

"I think that sounds wonderful. I didn't realize that I was starving until you brought up food," I commented before I walked back into the bungalow and brought out the blankets. "It'll be like a beach picnic. Great idea."

I meant it, too. There was something special and memorable about every moment. Once I had the blankets laid out and the food set up on it, we settled in to relax. "You really do look tired," I mentioned. "Eat." Then I fed him some grapes.

"What are you going to eat?" He asked.

"A little of everything," I said, reaching for a pickle, then sliding it in and out of my mouth intentionally.

Smirking, he said, "Nice."

Though I had intended for our conversation to stay light and playful, it soon turned. "What are you doing after the cruise?" He asked. "When the boat docks in Charleston, what does your future hold?"

Looking at him for a moment, I considered not answering. "I thought we were keeping this fun. That sounds like a serious question." Biting into a strawberry, I watched for a reaction.

Nodding, he said, "I could see how it would be perceived that way." Then he smiled. "You can't fault a guy for being curious. I mean…all I know about you is that you attract losers, yet have excellent taste in men when you don't overthink it." He winked. "I know that you are incredibly sexy, but have an equally intelligent mind. Do you blame me for wanting to get to know you better?"

Smiling carefully, I responded. "I guess not. I just thought we were following these rules."

"As I recall, the rules say nothing about not talking about our lives, just not contacting each other, or making it possible for us to contact each other, right?" He raised an eyebrow as he finished speaking.

The eyes did it. It was always his eyes that spoke volumes and broke down my defenses. It was going to be hard enough leaving this man behind. The more I knew about him, the more dangerous it became. With this conversation, I was truly biting the bullet…or maybe dodging bullets.

Sighing, I said, "We haven't planned that far. We're talking about moving to Vegas. It's a good time for us to go and live it up for a while, especially since it isn't the kind of place I would want to live forever."

Smirking, he shook his head. "Of course not. That's why the housing market crashed like it did there." He laughed. "So, you and Jolie."

"We always move together. We always have our own place, our own space, but when one of us requests a move, the other goes along. It's been like that since high school. We are living our dreams." I lay back, but turned my head to look at him still. "We have rules. Our life works for us."

"Have you ever considered settling down?" He asked, seemingly enthralled with the conversation.

"Hmmm, not yet. That's actually one of our rules: never settle and never settle down." I shrugged.

Lying on his back next to me so that we were shoulder to shoulder, he finally asked the one question I hoped to never have to consider. "What if you weren't settling?"

There it was. Sitting there, out in the open, like the white elephant on the beach. There had been times that thought had crossed my mind this trip. *What if Mr. BE was actually who I was supposed to be with? What if the move was to wherever he lived? What if it was time to settle down?* I mean…I was closing in on thirty…in a few years.

"What if I wasn't settling?" I repeated. "Well, first I'd have to find someone I was wildly compatible with inside and outside of the bedroom. I'd have to find someone who could put up with my crazy. Wherever would I find such a prize?"

That was one way to sidestep a question. After proudly answering a question with a question, I waited. He was up on his elbow once more, staring at me, considering all that I had said. We might as well have still been inside naked; the questions had the same effect. We were stripped bare at the moment. So much was riding on this…it was my future, his future, a potential for our future. It had become a classic standoff. I rolled onto my elbow, too. We each stared at our opponent, both of us understanding the importance of the next spoken words. Just as the silence threatened to become uncomfortable, he spoke.

"You make a valid point."

Before he could say any more, the ship horn sounded, warning us that it was time to catch a boat back. Without saying another word, we worked together to gather our belongings, pack up, and head to the beach area designated for pick-ups. We were quiet, each lost in thought, and why wouldn't we be. There was much to consider. Finding someone on a cruise was highly unlikely. It was a doomed situation. This…a vacation in general and a cruise in particular were ridiculously impossible places to find a mate. There was no way that life together off the ship would ever compare to life on the ship. It guaranteed disappointment. To even try it was relationship suicide. Look at us. We didn't even know each other's names.

"You've been deep in thought," he commented as we walked back to our stateroom to drop off the beach bag. Once that was done, he finally spoke his mind. "What are you thinking?"

Glancing at his wrist, I made up an excuse. "It's time for sushi." I wore my most playful look when I turned to him. "Wanna come with me?"

He chuckled. "Ah, yes. I forgot I suddenly eat sushi with just wasabi, right?" He watched me nod. "I can't believe you don't use soy sauce."

I looked at him seriously. "It's the salt, man. I puff up like a blow fish."

"Well, we can't have that." He placed his hand on my lower back as we left the room and headed back to the promenade deck. Pausing he asked, "Does wasabi not have salt?"

I tipped my head to the side as I considered this. "Nah. Too hot. Scares the sodium away. And it's a widely known scientific fact that if you eat food with heat…like wasabi or hot sauce…that you burn off all those calories." I nodded wide-eyed.

"You are making that up," he accused as he struggled to keep a straight face.

"Okay, so it's more of a theory than a fact. What I do know is that I use hot sauce and wasabi all the time and eat like a pig. That makes it a fact for me." Then I stopped in the hall, stood on my tiptoes, wrapped my arms around his neck, and said, "I love playing with you.

Emma Nichols

You are my favorite." With that, I kissed him on the nose, released, and walked to the nearest elevator, leaving him to stare after me. Oh, yeah. He still wanted me.

While we were eating sushi, I caught a couple staring at us. At first, I wondered at it, and then I stared back, too. Brazenly. They seemed to be about our age, late twenties, early thirties at most. The woman had smaller boobs than I did. She had a taller, thinner figure, whereas I tended to be curvier with a thin waist and flat abs. She nudged her husband and I knew they were going to walk over and talk to us.

"Do you trust me?" I asked Mr. BE. He looked confused. He hesitated. So, I spoke again. "Tell me you trust me and I'll make this the most memorable night of your life. Got it?" He nodded blankly. "Now, just follow my lead."

The couple sat down across from us at the table we had chosen across from the casino. The man spoke first and what he said earned him an elbow to the ribs from his wife. "So, is this your first cruise?"

I laughed. It was the maritime equivalent of 'do you come here often?' Never would such a lame statement move me.

The wife looked at him after the elbow. "Don't speak," she said seriously. He started to open his mouth, but she gestured a closing motion with her hand and he stopped.

I couldn't help myself. "Wow. I swear I saw that move on *The Dog Whisperer*." If they didn't like it, it didn't matter to me. I could make Mr. BE's night memorable with or without help.

Brushing her long blonde hair back from her face, she smiled, "That's where I discovered it. Works on men, too. You should try it some time." She smiled sweetly at my cruise husband.

"Yes, well, I never need to. He's perfect." I shrugged.

"No man is perfect," she argued as she studied him a minute. "Leaves the seat up."

Shaking my head, I said, "Nope."

"Leaves empty boxes in the pantry?"

I looked at him, but he really didn't seem the type. "Afraid not."

I could see she was going to just keep going, so I helped her out. "He helps out around the house, he's gainfully employed, he lets me have all the girl time I want," I said, looking at her meaningfully. "He always makes sure I come before he does. I get it when I want, where I want, how I want. Hell, we did it in the hot tub just the other night."

There it was. Match point.

Emma Nichols

Glancing at him, she eyed me, looking at the top of my sundress and my ample cleavage. "All the girl time you want, huh?" She asked licking her lips.

"Yes, but he's more of a joiner and I wouldn't have it any other way. Last time, we laid down some ground rules and he obeyed completely." I was afraid that the word 'obeyed' might have set him off, so I squeezed his leg reassuringly. He must have caught on because he began massaging my leg.

"Well, what are your rules?" She asked curiously.

"I tell you what," I began. "I've had enough sushi, and now I'm really ready to eat. If you care to join us in our stateroom, this is the number." I grabbed my eyeliner from my clutch and wrote it on the cocktail napkin that came with the sushi. Passing her the napkin, I said, "Oh, and you should know in advance, for the ladies it's P&P Day in the cabin."

"P&P Day?" She asked, but her eyes were sparkling.

"Yes, all I can wear inside the room today…panties and perfume. Be sure to dress appropriately. The dress code is in full force the minute you step inside our suite." Then I stood and began to walk after gesturing to Mr. BE to join me. I made sure he walked in front of me, after all, it was me that she needed to watch walk away.

Once we stepped off the elevator onto our floor, he turned and looked at me with wide eyes. "Oh my god," he began. "What have you done?"

Eyeing him curiously, I tried to decide if he was excited, apprehensive, or angry. Judging by his actions, the way he kept running a hand through his hair, it was a combination of the three. "Listen, they'll either come and we'll have a hot and sexy time, or they won't and we'll have a hot and sexy time. Either way, it's a win-win situation." I shrugged.

"I've never…" he began.

"Yeah, I can tell," I said with a slight smile. "Believe me, you have nothing to be ashamed of. You have nothing to worry about. Your skills are impressive, your size is shocking, and your stamina is without match."

"Okay, that much is true," he said. "I just thought marriage was sacred."

I stopped in front of the door to the suite. "Was it sacred when we had sex with Jolie?" I asked.

He looked stricken that I had said that out loud and in the hall. "Get in the room," he whispered loudly.

"I'm just saying…" I started. "And what about this…we aren't even really married!"

That last part hit him like a splash of cold water in the face. "Wow. It's easy to get caught up in these games, isn't it?" He asked meekly.

"Very," I said as I climbed into his arms. "Now we need to discuss our rules quickly because I'm pretty sure we will be having company soon."

All of fifteen minutes later, there was a knock on the door. She stood there in a bathrobe, while he wore the same polo shirt and khaki shorts he had on before. Mr. BE had opened the door and I was sitting on the edge of the bed with my legs crossed in his gift panties, wearing his gift perfume, after taking the world's fastest shower. She stood and stared at me a moment before dropping her bathrobe. Her husband was quick to pick it up.

His eyes widened when he saw me. BE just smiled proudly. I was his…for the next few days…and he knew it. She came over and sat next to me, close enough that we could touch. I waited until I saw her licking her lips again to speak. "So, you share your ground rules and I'll share ours."

Her eyes were focused on my boobs. I knew she was dying to touch them, play with them, and lick them. "We're pretty much soft swap," I said as I reached over, took her hand in mine, and placed it on my boob. "We do girl on girl play, anything goes. And when we play with couples, I can give blow jobs, hand jobs, anything, but penetration. My husband...well, I don't want him in any vagina but mine. Otherwise, anything goes."

Her eyes shot up and she continued to play and tug on my nipple. She even had the other hand working my other boob. It was rather nice. I could see, even out of the corner of my eye, that both men were getting erections. Her husband was looking uncomfortable, pushing it down. Mr. BE, however, was leaned against the wall, letting it just stand out and take center stage. How I wanted to walk over and free that cock. Instead, I decided to let him. "Babe, you can undress now," I suggested.

He did so, starting from the top. I loved the surprise of it, when he took off his shirt, the unexpected muscle definition, the smattering of hair below his belly button that made the most seductive happy trail. So I may have sighed happily, which resulted in him shooting me the best smile.

Next it was off with the shorts. The minute they fell to the floor and we caught sight of his cock straining against the boxer briefs, even to the point of pulling the top open a good inch, I heard our guests gasp. "Oh, and my husband...is straight."

Emma Nichols

"All I need to know is that he doesn't mind anal. I have to have that in me," she said. She was so excited that she was really playing hard with my nipples. I knew my panties were wet. I had to get this moving along.

"Sure," I said, "With a condom."

She snapped her fingers at her husband, who pulled out a handful of condoms from his pocket. "How would you like to begin?" She asked.

Lying back on the bed, I said, "My kitty needs some love."

That was all the encouragement she needed. She had given some orders, but all I knew was that she was between my legs, first fingering me, then pulling aside my thong to taste me. I had glanced over at Mr. BE. My need was great. No orgasm would be complete unless he was a part of it.

Swiftly, he moved from his position next to the closet to the side of the bed. I took him in my hand and started stroking him. Her husband had finally undressed and seemed to be servicing her, getting her ready for BE. Her poor husband, but I couldn't think about him. I loved every moment of making memories with BE.

Soon, he pulled away from my hand and my eyes shot open in worry. They shouldn't have. He stood there looking down at me. If I didn't know any better, I would have thought it was love that I saw. I mean, guys had professed their love plenty, but I had never really felt it back. Sure, there were some that I missed more than others, but no one had ever really been able to get under my skin. Ever. There he was, looking down at me with those eyes. I didn't know his name, but I knew that I would miss him in a way I had never missed anyone before.

Suddenly, he bent low, hovering over my lips with his, staring into my eyes with his amazing blue ones. "I have to tell you something," he said seriously. All I could do was nod in expectation. "I love you," he said seriously. "I really *really* love you." Then before I could respond, before I could even process what to say, he closed the distance between our lips and kissed me…deeply, passionately.

It sent me over the edge. In that moment, I had the first of many orgasms that night. It had little to do with the three sets of hands roaming over my body. It had nothing to do with the other couple that tried to please me by licking and sucking on my kitty. Yet it had everything to do with one man I hardly knew professing his love and giving me the most memorable kiss of my entire life.

I might just love Mr. BE.

Chapter 8

"About last night," he said as soon as I opened my eyes on Day Six of the cruise. Outwardly I cringed at his words, inside my heart was racing, my stomach was somersaulting, and my womb was pulsing. There was a lot going on at the moment.

"What about last night?" I asked as calmly as I could manage.

"I may have said some things in the heat of the moment…" he started.

"No take backs!" I shouted as I leapt from the bed. I stuck my fingers in my ears and rushed to the bathroom. Slamming the door behind me, I leaned against it. *Well, that went well,* I thought as I studied my reflection in the mirror. There was a bead of sweat over my lip. For some reason, I wanted to cry.

Those words he spoke last night, I didn't care if they were in the heat of the moment. I didn't care if he decided in the light of day that he felt differently. It mattered…to me, it mattered that I had his love. Even if I never saw him again, I wanted his love now.

Reaching behind the curtain, I turned the lever for the shower. While it warmed up, I brushed my teeth and studied my face objectively in the mirror. Did I look different? I felt different.

Finally as the mirror began to fog, I stepped in. By the time my hair was wet, I was no longer alone. BE had come up behind me.

"You misunderstood," he began quietly in my ear while he reached around and held me close to his wet naked form. "I shouldn't have said what I did with an audience. I never told you before. I should have waited until we were alone, in a moment like this."

I whipped around and looked at him wide eyed. "You aren't taking it back?" I asked, suddenly more ashamed than I had been even moments before when I rushed into the bathroom.

"No, I'm not taking it back, but I would like to do it right this time." He took a deep breath. "I love you, nameless wife. I love you like I have never loved anyone." He smiled at me in a way that made my toes curl. "For you, I would break all the rules." He leaned down and looked into my eyes, "All of them." Then he kissed me in a way that made my womb wish for things it never had before.

Over breakfast, we made our plans for the day in Nassau. "So, I've never been here before," he said. "Maybe we should just spend the day sightseeing."

"I have," I mentioned. "There's not a lot of sight to see. We can go to the flea market, the beach, that kind of thing. Honestly, the best part of

Emma Nichols

Nassau is Atlantis over on Paradise Island."

One thing I had noticed about him was that he never asked how much anything cost. He never complained about money. It was as though money were not an object. That was incredibly appealing. I had plenty of money. I could have paid my own way. I didn't beg for things. I didn't live beyond my means. That meant I had a very nice nest egg. Hell, it meant that every time I moved, I could buy a new nest. I had homes in cities all over the US rented by property management companies. My parents had trained me for financial success while they prepared me for college. I owed all of my success to them.

"So, we'll do that. I can't wait. We should be able to watch the sunset from there," he said with a smile.

We went back to the room before debarking to pack our bag. I knew what to expect there, so I was actually allowed to touch the bag. It was packed in minutes and we were debarking soon after that.

If yesterday was about romance and sexy time, today was about fun in the sun. A woman standing at dock offered to hook us up with a taxi as soon as we passed the welcome sign. We took her up on it and drove in one of the many dilapidated vans that doubled as taxis on the island. A short ten-minute ride later, we pulled up to Atlantis.

"What would you like to do first?" He asked.

Shrugging, I said happily, "Everything."

That's just what we did. It was fun. It was interesting. It was a learning experience.

For example, I learned to never comment that I had too much to carry. That could mean that we would have to go to the Gucci store next and pick out a new bag. Also, I should never joke when going through an aquarium filled with lobsters that I wanted to pick one out for dinner. That could result in us having a lobster dinner next to the same aquarium. Most of all, I should never comment that after a week with him, I was going to need a BOB to satisfy me.

"Who's Bob?" He asked with narrowed eyes.

Laughing, I responded, "Not a who…a what. BOB stands for battery operated boyfriend."

That had us picking out a few sex toys in one of the shops. It had me commenting, "Wow, they really do have everything here, don't they?"

Finally, our most expensive stop was the jewelry store. It wasn't like the duty free stores. They were like going to Wal-Mart compared to these places.

"Pick," he said, gesturing around the place. "Anything you want. It's yours. It's for tomorrow."

Emma Nichols

"Tomorrow?" I asked. Since it was the last day of the cruise, I was dreading it. This time, this magical period of my life would be over too soon.

"Yes." He took a breath, and then he grabbed my ring hand and held it to his lips as he kissed it while looking into my eyes. "See, P&P Day was created by a friend of mine. He and his girlfriend used to do that one day a week when they were off together. I always thought it sounded fun, if I could just find someone to do that with. Then I met you. Only…you are an original, one of a kind. We deserve a day of our design. Then, it came to me after our talk earlier."

"Oh, really?" I said, confused.

"Yup. Our day, tomorrow, will be B&B Day." He watched me for a reaction. I was busy trying out the initials in my head to no avail. Coming closer, he whispered in my ear, "Baubles and BOB."

I burst out laughing. "Perfect. You may have actually found a way to make me look forward to tomorrow," I said.

"You aren't? It's a full day at sea. We get to just *be* all day. Whatever we want to do. We don't even have to leave the room if we want. We could just order room service all day." He shrugged.

"Aren't there still things that we need to do? Boring things?" I smiled.

He thought for a moment before he asked me, "Like what?"

I leaned into his chest and wrapped my arms around his waist. "Promise not to laugh," I said.

"Of course not," he said. "Nothing is too boring, mundane or cliché for us. Got it?" He lifted my chin and forced me to look him in the eye.

"I want to see the sunrise with you. I want to watch the sunset. I want to make out during a movie. Silly, huh?" I tried to smile through the shame, but I couldn't do it. It was a weak smile at best.

"Baby, anything for you, but first…pick!" He urged.

By the time we left, I had a necklace with a diamond star and a matching bracelet. Rather than wear them out, we packaged them to go so that they would seem so special and new in the morning. From there, we walked through the resort until we reached the casino.

"Care to gamble?" He asked.

Shaking my head, I declined. "No, I never gamble. I don't mind watching. I've just learned that too many people risk more than they can lose. I do that enough in life, I don't need to risk money, too."

Looking at me, he frowned. "What do you have to lose?" He asked curiously.

Sighing, I admitted something I never expected to. "My heart," I said quietly. Then I walked on ahead alone, before he could lay his hand on my back or say something that would allow him deeper access to my already weakened heart.

When we returned to the ship, we dropped everything off in the suite before we headed to the buffet. "You bought us lobster dinners at Atlantis. What could you possibly still want to eat?" I asked him in shock.

"Dessert. There should always be room for dessert. I'm going to have some ice cream. Care to join me?" He asked offering me his arm.

"Oh, I'll join you. I just don't plan to eat. I need to watch my figure." I smiled at him.

"Baby, I've been watching it all week. You are perfect." Then he punctuated his proclamation with a kiss on the very tip of my nose. "Have some ice cream with me and then we'll do some boring stuff after?"

Narrowing my eyes, I asked, "Like what?"

"Like sunset. Better hurry," he said.

That was all the motivation I needed. We ate our ice cream on the back of the boat while watching the sun sink low over the ocean. After giving it some thought…I'm not sure there was a way we could have made it more special. It was absolutely perfect, just like that.

"I just want you to know…I've been paying attention," he said seriously as he led me to the Jubilee Lounge.

We found a sofa way up high in the back. "What are we doing here?" I asked.

"Just wait," he urged.

Minutes later, it happened. The screen opened up and a movie started. I don't remember it. Not any of it. I wasn't there for the movie. I was there for making out.

Man, did we make out. It was incredible. And when an older couple sitting near us looked at us disapprovingly, and a teenager suggested we get a room, we looked at each other, nodded and headed back to the room.

Time was too precious to waste. The promise of tomorrow was too great. We needed our rest. As he held me tightly in his arms once more, I couldn't help but get more than a bit nostalgic as I realized that I would only get to fall asleep like this one more time. There was a lump in my throat as I tried to fall asleep.

Chapter 9

The only evidence I had that I had fallen asleep was that I woke up. I felt as though a bus had hit me. The sleep had not been restful in the least. When I walked out on the balcony, I realized that it was raining. It seemed fitting. Not only did the rain make for a perfect excuse to stay in the cabin, but also it was as though the sky had opened up to mourn with me. BE was still asleep, resting peacefully. It was time for me to shake off the melancholy and get ready for what I hoped would be a wildly romantic day.

So I practiced smiling in the mirror while I waited for the shower to heat up. I shaved everything really well. I scrubbed my skin with the body scrub. After drying off, I applied lotion, I towel dried my hair, and I repainted my nails. Still, he slept.

Since breakfast was the most important meal of the day, I decided to get us food from the buffet. Leaving him a note on the pillow, I headed up to the lido deck. It didn't take long to gather our favorites. It took even less time to return to the room. He was just stirring in bed when I entered the stateroom.

"For you," I said, warmly. "Fuel up. I plan to burn a lot of calories today."

"Do you now?" He said with a still sleepy smile.

"Absolutely." I nodded. "I have big plans for you."

We ate breakfast in bed. Then, with satisfied bellies, we lay there and a natural series of conversations ensued. "What was your first time like?" He asked as he ran his hand up and down my side.

Smirking, I responded, "If you are asking if I've always been a nympho…I'm afraid so." I sighed. "It seems I was a bit naïve. My boyfriend picked me up on the Fourth of July to go to an amusement park about an hour and a half from home. When we arrived in the town, the weather suddenly turned and the sky opened up."

I began tracing his nipples with one finger. "So, after we killed time playing in an arcade, after we killed more time visiting souvenir stores, and finally after we had run out of options for killing time, we stopped at a drug store. He left me in the car as he ran inside. When he returned, just in time to avoid a ticket for being double-parked, he passed me a big paper bag. In it there were a dozen roses, some snack food, and a three pack of condoms."

He stared at me. "I'm listening," he prodded gently.

"From there we drove to a resort on the lake that had a bunch of cabins. Again, I was left in the car as he ran in. The whole time, I was trying to decide what to do. I wasn't sure I was ready. We hadn't been dating that long. At the same time, I was closing in on my seventeenth birthday. All my friends had already had lost their virginity. It had stopped seeming like this big prize, any big deal at all. So, when he brought me in and sat on the bed and said those magic words…we had sex." I shrugged.

"So, he told you he loved you and you had sex with him." He sounded partially amused, partially annoyed.

"No…not that," I said taken aback. "He told me that we didn't have to have sex, that we could just lay there all day and watch television. He told me he bought the condoms just in case, former Boy Scout and all. That sealed it. I liked his attitude. I reasoned that there couldn't be a more perfect first. And in the end I was right." I looked at him slyly. "Okay, my first was actually my first, second, and third."

"Ummm, how's that?" He asked.

"Well, I may have mentioned that I was inexperienced? I didn't realize that just because he purchased a three pack of condoms, didn't mean that we didn't need to use all of them." I peeked at him then. He was stifling a laugh.

"Wow, you were a teenage boy's dream, weren't you?" He leaned over me and kissed me repeatedly. Before I could say anything else, he added, "And now you're mine…my dream, my wish come true."

"I am?" I smiled brightly at him.

"Didn't you want to ask me? Did you want to know about my first time?" He asked.

"Me? Ask you?" I asked. Shaking my head vehemently, I assured him, "No, I don't want to know about your past. I don't want to know about anyone before me."

It was still raining after lunch. We had finally dressed and left the room, if only temporarily to get some fuel. "What do you want to do now?" He asked with a sparkle in his eye.

"Well, I think we should try out your B&B Day idea," I suggested.

"What are you more excited about…the baubles or the BOB?" He asked while wiggling his eyebrows.

Sighing, I said, "You know I'm not materialistic. So, the baubles while nice are completely unnecessary. Then there's the BOB…I have you, so what do I need it for?"

"Oh," he said, sounding a bit disappointed.

"But wait, there's more!" I joked. "At the same time, I love getting frisky with you. I love trying new things with you. This will be an amazing opportunity for us to make some memories."

With that said, we rushed back to the room. Fumbling with the card, he opened the door, turned to me, grabbed my face in his hands, and kissed me hard. "Time to get undressed," he said excitedly.

Walking through the door, I dropped my clothes one item at a time. By the time I reached the side of the bed, BE was sitting there holding open the jewelry case. "Time to get dressed, " he said sweetly.

"If you insist," I said, holding out my wrist. He attached the bracelet first, and then I turned around so he could affix the necklace. Once that was in place, I stood and waited.

Slowly, he opened the black bag. I was dying to know all the contents. He claimed to have thrown in a few extras. Eager was not even touching on how excited I was to discover what would happen next. BE stood and walked towards me with something in his hand. When he opened it, I realized it was a blindfold.

Without thinking, I shivered. There was something really sexy about a blindfold. Without being able to see, he could do anything. I wouldn't be able to do anything but feel and anticipate.

"There," he said after he covered my eyes. Then he took me by the hand and led me to the bed. I started to climb onto the bed, but he stopped me, halted my progress. "Wait," he commanded.

Soon, I was bent over. He was running his fingers slowly down my back, caressing my buttocks. Every touch had me on fire. The scent of cinnamon explained it. He was rubbing heated flavored massage oil all over. When he lay me down on my back and started massaging my boobs, I thought I was going to lose it. That was too much. I started moaning and writhing in ecstasy. Then one thought occurred to me…*what if he used that on my vag?*

Moments later, I didn't have to wonder since his fingers were searching, stroking, and touching my most sensitive region. My pelvis rose and fell with his attention. "In me, please," I begged, remembering how successful that was last time I had used it. Only this time, he seemed less than interested in giving in to me.

"Patience, beautiful," he urged. "I want to take my time. I'm searing every bit of this into my memory. I hope you are, too."

The bed sank near me and I knew that he had finally decided to join me. I reached out to feel him and discovered that he, too, was naked. Lacing my hand through his, I squeezed him affectionately before I brought his fingers to my mouth to suck and lick. Hearing him inhale sharply brought a wicked smile to my face.

"Did you think that by blindfolding me you had incapacitated me?" I asked haughtily. "You didn't. You enhanced the pleasure for sure, but I don't need eyes to see you. I can find you with my hands." At that pronouncement, I proceeded to run my hands all up and down his chest. In my mind, after studying him in similar situations, I didn't have to see his face. I had memorized it, every expression, every action, and I knew just what to do to elicit the reaction I desired.

He was on his back and easily enough I managed to climb on top of him, rub some of the excess oil from my body and transfer it onto his. Only, I took it a step further. When I had slowly rubbed it around his nipples and I could tell it was taking effect based on his reaction, I leaned down slowly, pursed my lips together, and blew a cool breath over first one, then the other.

Since he could see, I knew that he had watched each move as I made it. He had given away his excitement in his ragged breathing. He had told me how amazing my actions felt by the sharp intake of breath. Now, as my wet vag hovered over his rock solid cock, I could feel him quivering, just a little bit.

Instead of letting him in, I rubbed my wet folds up and down the entire steely length of him again and again until he grabbed my waist and flipped me over, off him, onto the bed. Since I was on my stomach already, I simply assumed the position and pushed my ass high in the air. That's when I heard it: the vibrator.

He had looked at multiple sizes and styles. Finally, thinking his new obsession was bordering on the unhealthy, I had left the store to find a bathroom while he finished making his purchase. He had done well, so far. In a matter of seconds, I should know how well he had done here, too.

Surprisingly enough, I didn't feel much of anything besides his finger inside me. Then it started vibrating. The intensity was enough to make me whimper. "A bullet," I murmured.

Then ever so slowly, he entered me from the back. While some women took offense to this position, citing that they preferred to see their partner, I liked this method. I loved feeling the man slam into me, his balls slapping against me. I loved when a man would reach around and rub my clit while sliding in and out, or rub my nipples with a palm. This moment was as close as I had ever been to heaven.

The day continued like this. Eventually, I lost the blindfold and I could see him once more. I think he missed looking in my eyes as much as I missed looking in his. Our B&B Day was flowing along nicely. We had even introduced a few games. There was a body bingo board game that helped us extend the foreplay and touching when all I wanted was to get to the main event. There were sex dice that also encouraged us to try new things on various body parts.

We napped before our final dinner. By now we had learned that the only games for us were the ones played in the bedroom. Instead of even speaking to others, we were so wrapped up in each other that no one else could entice us into a conversation. There was no other woman stroking his arm, no other man stroking my ego. We ate, sharing food off of our plates. We drank, sharing a bottle of wine that the maître d' suggested.

Finally, we headed back to the room. While we were out, the customs paperwork had been slid under our door. A towel animal graced our bed.

"What is that?" He asked.

Taking a second look, I replied, "I believe it's a snail. Must be a reminder for you to take your time with me tonight," I joked.

"Oh, I planned on it," he said seductively. "I hope you don't plan on sleeping."

I shrugged. "Jolie can drive us back to Raleigh."

So part two of our B&B Day began. It wouldn't end at midnight. It wouldn't end at dawn. The reality was that once it was over, it really was the end. We wanted it to last as long as possible.

We played an extended version of truth or dare coming dangerously close to breaking our rules. We played with rabbit. We worked with a cock ring. I wore my first vibrating nipple clamps. He pulled out some bonus gift that had been thrown in for making such a huge purchase. It was a set of anal beads. We laughed and stuck them back in the bag.

Finally, he pulled out a red satin rectangular box with a black bow on it. "These are for you," he said. "I figured you might need them after this week."

Looking at him curiously, I slowly lifted the spring-loaded lid. When it snapped fully back, it exposed a pair of glass lotus Ben Wa balls. "I've never used these before," I said. "They are so pretty."

"Well, your pretty kitty deserves nothing less. Let's take these babies for a test drive." With that, he took the box from my hand and slowly removed them. "Lay back for me," he said calmly.

Doing as he requested meant that a moment later he had inserted first one, then the other ball into my vagina. After that, he inserted himself into my vagina, too. Somehow, that was even hotter, even better than previous times. The experience was so intense for me that it had him pausing to question. "Are you in pain? Is this too much? Am I hurting you?" A worried frown blanketed his face.

"No," I said shaking my head. "All that hurts…is my heart."

He stopped thrusting into me once more. While he was frozen in place, I rolled him over and took top. "There's something I have to tell you," I began. Swallowing slowly to try and dislodge the lump in my throat, I said something I've never said to a single soul…or at least not to anyone I'm not related to by blood. Brushing the hair back from his face, I leaned low. I hovered over his lips as he had done to me so many times over the past few days. "I love you," I said.

I had played it over in my head, practiced it several times since he had made his announcement. Mostly, I had wondered what it would feel like. Was I losing some power by admitting my feelings? Was I making myself vulnerable? Would this admission be the end of me? Was I now going to turn into some sappy girl?

Only…nothing bad came of it. I could have sworn that I saw tears in BE's eyes. It was hard to say since he crushed his lips to mine as soon as I finished speaking. There was a moment that the kissing stopped, that we were frozen there, nose to nose, attached at the pelvic region, and all I wanted to do was stay there forever.

All morning, I had played out in my head how I would explain all of this to Jolie. I knew what she would say, what I could expect of the conversation on the way home. She would ask me how I knew it was love. How could I love him when I have never loved anyone before? The best I could figure…it was love; it was real because it made absolutely no sense…logically. Yet as I looked at it from every other angle, how could I not love him…this man who rescued me, who protected me, who spoiled me, and treated me like I was absolutely precious to him.

We napped some in between lengthy lovemaking sessions. Around 5am, we took a shower together, lovingly washing and caressing each other's most sensitive areas. We dressed in silence and while I can't vouch for him, I know that my silence was a product of fear. I had no idea what I might say next, what I might reveal.

"Time to go," he said simply.

I froze, completely stricken. "Already?" I asked sadly.

Glancing at the ship's information station on the television, he nodded. "We need to get going if we are to watch that sunrise together. That and breakfast…our last two boring activities together."

Placing his hand on my lower back, he led us out the door. It was bittersweet, this moment of watching the sunrise while accepting that it signaled an end to our time together. We stopped at the buffet to pick up a hot tea for me and a coffee for him. I put in extra sugar because I needed it. We walked out onto the deck and found the perfect spot to watch the sun slowly rise up over the horizon.

The sky turned from pinks and purples to oranges. The sun was a flaming orange ball. The sky was clear, the air smelled clean and fresh after a day of rain. I felt fresh, too. Only just as I was ready to try something new, that opportunity was slipping away from me.

We went inside just as the buffet opened. "Let's eat," he suggested. "We can pick a table by the window and talk before it gets too crazy in here."

Emma Nichols

Numbly, I nodded and allowed him to direct me through the line and the ever-growing crowd of people entering to get in one last meal before the last debarking. With heaping plates, we sat apart from the crowd. We ate in silence, the tension of the approaching departure weighing on both of us.

BE took my hand in his, touched the ring one last time, and admired the bracelet on that wrist. "You know," he began slowly, "some rules are stupid and don't make any sense. Yours, for example." He looked me straight in the eye suddenly and from somewhere inside me sprang a glimmer of hope. "At the same time, I want to respect your wishes." That same hope died.

He sighed. "So, maybe a compromise is in order?"

Slowly, a smile spread across my face. Part of me wanted to jump up and down while screaming *Yes! Yes! Yes!* Then I remembered I was an adult, so I said, "What do you have in mind?"

"How soon could you move to Vegas?" He asked. I could tell that he was making some mental calculations.

It was time for me to do some of my own. I could have the movers come, load up the house, hire a property management company, a cleaning service, pack a few necessities and be on my way, just as soon as I helped Jolie do the same. She always needed an extra push. "A week," I said. "I could be there in a week." The more I considered it, the more confident I became.

With a sparkle in his eyes, he asked, "What if we were to meet in Vegas in a week?"

Biting my lip, I knew I would accept that proposal, just like I had accepted the last. I nodded. Then a thought crossed my mind. "We don't even know each other's names. How will I ever find you?"

"Simple," he said confidently. "We met on a boat, we'll meet for a boat ride." He was playing with my hand now, caressing it, squeezing it in the most distracting way.

"Yeah, I don't understand." I shook my head.

He leaned in. "Meet me at the gondola ride in the Venentian at 7pm next Saturday. I'll be waiting for you. I promise."

Over the years, I had suffered through a lot of broken promises. This time was different. This man, I believed. This plan, I didn't doubt for a moment. The week apart would quickly pass. Then we'd be together in Vegas.

Sure, there were a lot of unanswered questions. They would stay that way. Those questions were for another time, another trip: our visit in Vegas. All that mattered was that today wasn't goodbye.

Glancing at his watch BE said simply, "Let's get you back to Jolie."

Emma Nichols

I nodded. Everything felt different now. I could walk away from this intact. I wouldn't need to cling or cry. One week would be a very short time.

With my key, we didn't have to knock. As soon as I opened the door, I found Jolie just walking out of the bathroom with her armload of toiletries. "You're back," she said happily.

"Do I get any credit for returning her in one piece?" BE asked.

"I don't know. Did you give her lots of orgasms like you promised?" She asked with her hands on her hips.

Placing a hand over his heart he said solemnly, "I am a man of my word."

We didn't have time for long lingering goodbyes. Instead, I kissed him like I was going to see him later, just like he promised. "Saturday, 7pm, The Venetian gondola ride," he said holding both my hands in his. "I'll see you then." After another quick kiss, he turned and walked away.

"So, you broke your rules?" Jolie asked with an approving smile.

"Not yet," I said. "I will in Vegas. That's the kind of town where rules are meant to be broken." I smiled at her as I watched her pack.

"As long as it's just rules and not your heart," she said happily. "So, Sin…next stop: Vegas?"

I nodded. "I'll be his Vixen in Vegas."

She threw an arm around my shoulders. "Sin City, here we come."

Vixen in VEGAS

Emma Nichols
Copyright 2013. Emma Nichols

Available Now!

I am not a gambler. I don't make bets…not on sports, not in casinos. I don't take unnecessary chances. There will be no bungy jumping, no skydiving, no parasailing. When it comes to making decisions in my life, I weigh the odds, consider my skillset, and decide from there. There are some risks that I'm willing to take, calculated risks, the ones that don't scare me at all. Working online, being self-employed, moving whenever the mood strikes me…. these have never felt like risks. These decisions always felt like the natural progression for me.

Real estate is a gamble that I've never lost. My choices have served me well. At the tender age of 28, I have five properties in five different states. Four of them are rented. The fifth, I'm living in…for a few more days. As I drive back to Raleigh from Charleston, I'm completely lost in thought. Never before have I taken a chance when I have stood to lose more than I could safely. So what the hell was I doing…laying my heart on the line? Lost in thought, I was zigzagging impatiently through traffic.

"You do realize that the week won't go any faster just because you drive faster, right?" Jolie asked, jolting me from my thoughts.

"What?" I asked, without even considering what she had said.

"Slow down! If you kill us, you'll never get to Vegas," she urged.

Glancing down at the speedometer, I realized that I was pushing 90mph. Crap. With a loud sigh, I took my foot off the accelerator and gave her an apologetic frown. "I'm sorry, girl. I wasn't paying attention."

Reaching over to pat my arm, Jolie smiled sympathetically. "I know," she said. "I get it. There is a lot to do over the next few days. Are we driving or flying to Vegas?"

My face scrunched up in thought. I felt it and stopped myself. No need to do more damage than time already was. "Wow. I really haven't thought this through. We've never moved so quickly before. I mean, I have to call the realtor and have them find a renter for the house. I have to call PODS and get a few storage containers. Then there's turning off all the utilities, returning the cable box, putting a hold on the mail." I shook my head it was spinning so hard.

Chuckling, Jolie calmly pulled out her iPhone. "Let's make a list," she

Emma Nichols

said simply.

I marveled at her, sounding so calm when I felt like my head might just freaking pop off. "Look at me. I'm a wreck. This isn't me. What happened?" I raised my hand, exasperated and utterly disgusted with myself.

"Love," she said seriously. "My baby finally found love." With that declaration, she turned her attention to the new note she was creating.

Something in me calmed down. I could do this. We could do this. In a week, I'd be starting a new life in Vegas. If he kept his word, Mr. BE would be there, with me, a part of this new life. That…*that* was what had me all unhinged.

I don't do love. Only now…with BE, maybe I did. All I knew for certain was that one week wasn't enough. We had more story to tell, more life to live, more experiences to be had. He made me feel things in a way I never had before. He made me want things I had never wanted…like permanence. Shoot, I might even consider breaking all my rules for him.

For this man, I would settle down because I sure as hell didn't feel like I was settling. He was everything I never knew I always wanted. We knew practically nothing about each other and yet…we made sense. Somehow, I didn't care about his past. All I thought about now was our future. I just needed to survive this week. A lot of that was going to depend on the list.

Slowly, I inhaled and exhaled a few times. I set the cruise control on the SUV. Finally, when I felt more relaxed, I spoke to Jolie once more. "So, how is that list coming along?"

Nodding, she looked up at me and smiled widely. "We're good. It's all good. You know how this works. We've done this so many times before. It doesn't even matter that we are on a time schedule. We've got this."

Without saying another word, Jolie picked up my phone and started to place a call. "Here," she said, "tell the nice lady about your house."

Blowing out another breath, I reached for the phone and began the conversation that would start it all. We were really doing this. We had done this before, but this time…it was more real. This move was the scariest move ever.

We stopped soon after that phone conversation. Something about a week on the cruise ship had conditioned my body into thinking it needed to be fed every few hours. Smiling to myself, I realized that some of that had to do with the fact that I had burned a heck of a lot of calories on that trip. This was going to be a long week. At the end of it, we will have spent as much time apart as we had together.

Emma Nichols

The chocolate shake from the McDonalds drive thru was just what I needed to tide me over for the rest of the drive. That…and the chicken wrap. Somehow, because it was chicken, I had managed to trick my body into believing it had just eaten something healthy. Sucker. The shake was drink and dessert all in one cup, with whip cream and a cherry on top. I smiled lazily as I drove.

"When is the realtor coming to look at the place?" Jolie asked. She didn't have a house to rent. In Raleigh, she had opted to rent an apartment. She didn't expect for us to be here as long as we were. Three years was a long time for us. Before that, it had been a couple of years max in each of the other states.

What she had failed to consider was that Raleigh was so close to everything…the beaches, the mountains, other major metro areas. We had spent countless afternoons walking trails and taking pictures. Please note I said walking…I don't hike. If I can't do it in my flip-flops, I don't do it. My toes hate being confined. As cute as they are with a pedicure, that would just be wrong anyway.

Living in Raleigh had meant years of photo opps. There were plenty of famous people passing through, plenty of festivals to attend, and plenty of scenic areas to capture. Raleigh was incredibly profitable. Now we were gearing up for our new adventure.

"Well, the realtor is coming at 10am on Monday, so I guess I have two days to work on packing and cleaning," I said with a sigh. "Jolie, how am I going to do this?"

"I only have an apartment to pack. I can help you. You can hire a cleaning service. The movers will pack for you if you can just decide to go that route instead of a storage container. This is easy," she chided.

"Not that...BE," I murmured. "I don't know how to do it. Clearly I suck at relationships. Look at Kyle. Look at every guy before him."

"They don't count. And whatever you did over the past week obviously works, right?" Jolie said gently.

"Okay." I took a few breaths. "I'm done."

"What do you mean you're done?" She looked more alarmed than anything.

"No more freaking out. I'm not even going to think about it. I'm just going to keep my head on the move. Next Saturday I'll see him and we'll take it from there." I nodded my head. That was that.

It was early afternoon when I dropped Jolie back at her apartment. She grabbed her bag, leaned in, and gave me a quick peck on the cheek before she walked away. I pulled out of the apartment complex and drove the short drive to my house in what is really considered Cary, North Carolina. My little Cape at the end of the cul-de-sac looked lonely and neglected. The mailbox was full. The grass was long. Since I had left after dark, all the blinds were closed.

Because of Mr. BE's generosity, I needed to make more than one trip into the house. I started to unpack all the clothes. Instead, I decided to only take out the dirty clothes for washing. It didn't make any sense to do anything more than that. That's why I finally decided to just do it, just start some laundry, just run the dishwasher, just clean the fridge, do all those undesirable tasks that will make it possible for me to pack my house.

Before I had even finished, I heard that chime, the one that let me know I had a new text message. I hated that for a moment, my heart thudded in my chest as I rushed to check it. I knew…I *knew* that he didn't have my number, my name, anything. I knew that there was no way for him to contact me, but I so wanted him to find a way. The screen lit up as I slid my finger across. It was Jolie, forever faithful, always looking out for me, sending the To Do list we had created in the car.

That was almost as good. Let's face it; my head was everywhere. I needed her direction. I was too distracted to do this on my own. Putting on my game face, I opened the list to get to work.

By 7pm, I was too tired too cook. I should have ruled that out while cleaning the fridge anyway. I called for Chinese. It was a delivery kind of night.

By 8pm, I had folded all the laundry, packed all but a few outfits for the suitcase, and finally settled in to eat the food the delivery driver left. There was nothing on television. I wasn't going to miss that box once the movers arrived. I felt completely strange in my own skin. I didn't feel like me. I was unsettled. I was irritable. I was completely losing it. This was going to make for a long night.

Finally, I gave in and placed a call. It rang twice before she answered. I knew what to expect.

"What's up, babe?" Jolie asked lazily.

"I'm bored. Let's meet for a drink," I suggested.

"Where do you want to go?" She questioned, her interest piqued.

"Someplace close and quiet. What about that Irish pub down the road?" I asked seriously.

"Yup. Meet you there in twenty minutes." Jolie happily agreed.

After I ended the call, I puttered around the house, struggling to find something to do to kill time. I toyed with the idea of touching up my makeup, but really...I had no interest in anyone but BE. I didn't care about being attractive...I had no interest in attracting anyone. Really, I mostly wanted to be left alone. I shouldn't even be meeting Jolie. I just wanted a distraction so badly.

Sighing, I headed into the bathroom to get ready. Without thinking, I threw my hair up into a messy bun. Studying my face for a moment, I decided to go light and natural with the makeup despite the darkened bar. I was sun kissed. It if hadn't been for the look in my eyes, I'd have been really happy with my appearance. I was the picture of health. And the long flowing white sundress completed that image. With a sigh, I slid my feet into a pair of sandals.

For a moment, I considered my jewelry, but I knew in my heart I wasn't going to change it. I had been wearing the jewelry BE gave to me...the blue diamond ring and band, the bracelet and necklace. There were so few tangible ways for me to feel connected that I wasn't about to take them off. When I looked at my ring finger, it always made me smile.

Locking the door behind me, I headed to my vehicle parked in the driveway. Sure, I had a garage, but I never parked in it. It was just as well, since I would soon be filling it with boxes in anticipation of the move. Sliding behind the wheel, I started the SUV and headed to pub we had agreed to meet at. I was late. Jolie was used to that. There was some comfort in knowing that she would have staked out a table by the time I arrived.

Sure enough, after I parked and exited the vehicle, I found her in one of the little booths just inside the doorway. She lifted one hand absent mindedly as she waved my direction. She was on the phone, talking animatedly. When I sat across from her, she rushed to get off the phone. "Yeah, talk to you soon. Bye!" Turning her attention to me, she said, "What up, bitch?"

"Not much," I said. "I'm just…out of sorts."

A server stopped by the table then. The guy was cute, I guess. From his actions, I was certain he was used to women falling all over him. Poor guy. He wasn't going to be able to flirt his way to a fat tip tonight. I was impervious to the charms of other men and Jolie…lesbian.

"What can I get for you, gorgeous?" He asked, flashing a huge smile that exposed perfectly white straight teeth.

"Just a Coke for me," I said. Then I turned my attention once more to Jolie.

She rolled her eyes so hard, her entire head bobbed. "Please. And we need some Irish Nachos…extra sour cream." She studied the appetizers a moment more before shrugging and conceding. "And that should do it…but I reserve the right to order a brownie sundae later." She nodded and smirked.

My eyebrows rose. "A brownie sundae? Since when?"

"Since you are in mourning," she announced.

"I'm not in mourning! What do I have to be upset about? We just returned from an amazing cruise. I had some of the hottest sex of my life. And I'll be seeing him again in a week!" I crossed my arms over my chest. "We're starting a new adventure. Life is good."

"Yes, life is good, but you don't really believe that. This is why you are so out of sorts. You are having doubts. I can see it." She frowned at me.

"How would you know?" I sniffed. "I never have doubts. I am the picture of confidence." I leaned back in the booth in an attempt to project a picture of calm and cool.

She laughed at me then, a big hollow sound, the mocking one. "I've known you forever. The last ten years it has been the two of us and your flavor of the month. This guy, BE, he's not a flavor of the month. BE is the spice of life. You know it, and I know it. I know how unsettling this is for you. Just know that he won't let you down. He's not going to stand you up. You can focus on doing what needs to be done and soon, you will be together again."

"We'll see," I said with a shrug, trying to brush it off like it didn't matter. Oh, but the girl in me wanted to beg Jolie for more...more reassurance, more pretty words that would soothe my tortured soul.

Thankfully, the server returned with my drink and our food. Irish nachos are really just glorified potato skins. I stared at them for a moment, heaped with sour cream, topped with green onions, loaded with bacon, melted cheese and a tub of salsa for dipping. Jolie dug right in. I loved that about her, the way she was just so open and honest and real.

"Eat," she ordered, a hand covering her full mouth. She swallowed. "Damn these are good. Eat! It's comfort food. I ordered this with a purpose." She pushed the plate towards me.

With yet another sigh, I slowly reached out and transferred a few potato skins to my plate. Opening my napkin and releasing my silverware, I slowly cut up tiny bites and began to eat. Chewing pained me. Food lacked taste. And more than anything, I was pissed with myself for behaving this way and not being able to snap out of it. Gah.

"Good girl," Jolie said as she reached across the table and patted my hand a few times. She was smirking at me. "Depressed is a lousy look for you. Snap out of it. Pull yourself together. You don't want him to take one look at that sad face and run the other direction, right?"

Slowly, a smile spread across my face. It was the thought of seeing him again. Stupid heart. Stupid feelings. Stupid me for letting a man I don't know get under my skin. "Okay," I said. I took a deep breath then exhaled slowly. "I've got this. It's a week. Less."

"That's my girl," she said. The tension seemed to dissipate after that. I felt better. I really did. We talked business…all the cool new opportunities for us in Vegas. We talked about the move. We managed to carefully avoid talking about BE.

"Let's just check into the Venetian while we house hunt. Are you house hunting or are you getting an apartment again?" I asked.

"I'd like to get a house here. What about you? You should probably rent until you and BE figure things out," she said casually.

There it was. My stomach knotted. "I hate this. I don't like having my life up in the air. Right now…it is," I groaned.

Studying me for a moment, she folded her hands in front of her. Then turning her head, she motioned for our server. He must have been nearby because he was beside the table in a heartbeat.

"What can I get you?" He asked with that same smile.

"We're going to need a brownie sundae. Two spoons. Thanks," she said.

He scampered off to get the sundae and I gave her a feeble smile. "Wow. I must be in worse shape than I thought," I said.

When I returned home that night, I walked into the bedroom and left a trail of clothes on the way to the tub. I had splurged some when I updated this house. It had great bones. I loved just about everything about the old place, but I needed to bring it out of the fifties, make it more sellable. So, I gutted the kitchen when there were too many rainy days one spring. I couldn't get out and take pictures as I had hoped. I didn't feel like getting wet. I hated umbrellas. That's why I stayed in…and tugged at a loose piece of wallpaper. I just wanted to know what was under it. Three layers later, I discovered that the sheetrock hadn't even been primed. The end result was that tore everything out down to the studs, ran a new water line for the fridge, moved gas lines for the stove, installed new plumbing for the dishwasher, and designed my dream kitchen. I had always wanted a farmhouse sink, and now I had one. I had always said I'd try Silestone instead of going with the same boring granite every other home had. Oil rubbed bronze was my finish of choice. Because I needed everything to match…the project just grew from there, until I had matching tile in the bathroom and a nice deep Jacuzzi bath to go with my multi-head shower.

Finally the home felt like my own. I had increased the value immensely while making it more livable. Like I said, real estate was not a risk for me. It made sense. My choices felt right. My decisions came naturally…until now.

That's why I drew a bath. I soaked as long as I dared while listening to music that poured in from the bedroom. At last, I thought I might be relaxed enough to sleep. So, I did. I went to bed. The exhaustion had taken a toll. I fell hard and fast, just like I had for BE.

Soon, I found myself in this nightmare. I don't know how it started. I don't remember all of it. What I do remember is that BE never showed. I waited for him. I waited and refused to leave. I was completely pathetic. The gondolas closed. The hotel told me that I couldn't sleep there that I had to have a room. I did have a room, but I was afraid of missing him. What if he showed up and I wasn't there? There was no way for him to find me. None. We had no phone numbers. We had no emails. We couldn't be in touch. This…loving him…was the scariest thing I had ever done.

When I woke with a start, I felt it. My heart hurt. There was this overwhelming sadness that had taken hold. It was too much. My eyes were watering. Okay…fine. They were tears. Happy? I was crying. What the hell was I crying over? It was stupid. I was stupid. Never would I let a man make me feel this way, all scared and weak.

Grabbing for my phone, I sent Jolie a quick text.

Me: I'm done with this. I'll go to Vegas when I feel like it. If I bump into him, cool. I don't want to feel this way anymore. Talk to you in the morning.

Then I slammed my phone down on the nightstand. I threw my legs over the side of the bed. It was 4am. It was so ridiculously early…or late, depending upon the time zone. My bathrobe was lying at the foot of the bed, right where I left it after the bath. Slipping into it, I headed out to the kitchen. I didn't know what I wanted, really, but this seemed like the kind of moment in the movies where the sad, lonely pathetic chick would get all introspective over a cup of tea. I could get into that.

The water was just starting to boil when my phone rang. I rushed to the bedroom because…well, how often does a phone ring jut after 4am? It could be an emergency. It could be a prank call. Or, according to the picture that glowed on my screen, it could be Jolie calling to cheer me up. That warmed me instantly.

"Hey, girl," I said, all out of breath from my sprint for the phone. You may recall, I am not a jogger.

"Hey, sexy," he breathed into the phone.

It took me a minute to process just whom I was speaking to. Then the tears started. Actually, it was more of a waterfall effect. Then came the snot. "Oh my god! It's YOU! And you're on Jolie's phone!" I started sniffling while I wiped away the tears and tried my best to hold myself together.

"Yes, babe. It's me. Jolie called me. It's a three way. You know. Again," he joked.

I giggled.

"Are you crying?" He asked concerned.

"No," I lied. "Must be a cold."

"Good, I don't want you crying, especially when I can't be there to comfort you." He spoke soothingly into the phone and it reminded me of all those nights snuggled in his arms, talking, and making love. "What's going on? One day apart and you've already decided not to meet me?" He asked.

My chest constricted. It hurt so much. My voice caught in my throat. "I don't know how to do this. I've never done this before," I whispered hoarsely.

"What? You've never made plans a week in advance? You've never moved?" He asked questions he already knew the answers to just to make me think.

"I've never been in love," I admitted. "I'm scared of losing me to be with you." I was silent after that admission. It took a lot for me to share that.

"Well, if it makes you feel any better…I don't make a habit of falling in love. I tried it once. It didn't go the way I expected. I've been a little gun shy ever since. For you, I'd take a bullet. You are a once in a lifetime kind of love," he said quietly. "Promise me, you'll meet me."

This conversation was what I needed. Jolie had found the perfect way to soothe my soul and settle my nerves. No wonder she was my BFF. "Hmmm. I suppose I could promise you," I began playfully, "but what good are promises with you? Here we are, talking on the phone…"

"I'll have you know I thought this through. I've broken no rules. *You* don't have my name or my contact information. Jolie does. So there." He chuckled at his own cleverness.

I couldn't help but laugh. "And you think this information is safe with Jolie? You think I couldn't get it from her if I wanted?" I asked.

His deep sexy voice responded, "Yes, that is precisely what I think. Jolie loves you. Jolie even seems to be rather fond of me and she thinks we make a phenomenal couple. So let's stick to our rules for now. And when I see you on Saturday, you'll discover what a big, bad rule breaker I am. Just wait for me until then. If one of us needs to, we have Jolie to reach out for us." He was silent for a moment. So was I as I considered all he had said. "I love you, baby," he said. "Saturday, I'll be waiting for you."

Emma Nichols

"Saturday," I murmured. "I'm going to rock your world."

"Babe," he said seriously, "you already have."

About the Author

What made **Emma Nichols** decide to be an erotica author?

Simple.

How else was she going to parlay her two favorite past times into a career?

Emma is single and loving it. Like her first character, Alysin, Sin for short, she doesn't believe in settling or in settling down. She loves to indulge in her passions whenever the mood strikes and enjoys keeping all of life's cliché moments spicy.

Known for her sense of humor, Emma surrounds herself with friends whose antics often become the source of book fodder. Her ideal situation would be to explore the Caribbean while writing. She pursues that dream daily.

Fan her on Facebook (https://www.facebook.com/pages/Emma-Nichols/244344445704798), follow her on Twitter (http://twitter.com/EmmasErotica), and fan her on Goodreads (http://www.goodreads.com/author/show/7084178.Emma_Nichols).

Emma Nichols

Acknowledgements

Special thank you to JB McGee and Indie Pixel Studios…how many times did you save my butt on this book? I lost count. What matters is that I'm so lucky to work with you. Thank you for sharing your gifts with me.

Leanne Jacobson…thank you for donating your time to furthering my dreams. I appreciate you more than you will ever know.

Tammy Sipes…thank you for reading outside of your genre just because you wanted to help. You are stuck with me. Thank you, Beta Extraordinaire and friend.

Lorraine Masterson…you are my graphics queen! I totally heart you and appreciate all the extra work you do.

Team Nick's Chicks…thank you for taking on double duty, for cheering on and promoting two authors, for never complaining and always complimenting. So lucky to have all of you in my life. I'll make you proud. Promise!

To all my bloggers…Kathy, Brandelyn, Jennifer, Maria, Wendy, Brandy, Tanya, Renee and so many more of you…thank you for promoting, for reading, for working with the new kid.

Made in the USA
San Bernardino, CA
09 June 2014